Prentice Hugh

Frances Mary Peard

Alpha Editions

This edition published in 2024

ISBN 9789362092731

Design and Setting By
Alpha Editions
www.alphaedis.com
Email - info@alphaedis.com

Contents

Preface.

There are differences of opinion as to Bishop Bitton's share in the transforming of Exeter Cathedral, and I have followed that expressed by Archdeacon Freeman, who, after speaking of the prevalent idea that the present choir was the work of Stapledon, states that, from the evidence of the Fabric Rolls, it was done by Bitton, whose episcopate lasted from 1292 to 1307. After noticing the facts which point to this conclusion, Archdeacon Freeman adds: "We thus establish, as I conceive, with absolute certainty, the date of the completion of the *eastern half of the choir*, a point entirely misconceived hitherto. To Bitton and not to Stapledon it must be ascribed. And we shall see reason presently for ascribing to him all the substantial features of the remainder, and the vaulting of the whole."

With regard to the story itself, no one can be more conscious than I am myself of the dangers inseparable from attempting to place it at so early a date, when the author is at once plunged into a very quagmire of possible anachronisms. I can only ask the indulgence of those who, happening to cast their eyes upon these pages, detect there the errors in manners and customs which I am too conscious may exist.

It may be convenient, for the unlearned, to notice that the value of coins was about fifteen times as much as in the present day. Thus one pound equalled fifteen pounds, and one mark (or shilling) fifteen shillings. A groat contained four silver pennies, and there were two hundred and forty pennies in a silver pound.

Chapter One.

At Stourbridge Fair.

"Have at him, Peter!"

"Roll him in the mud!"

"Nay, now, 'twere rarer sport to duck the lubber in the river!"

These and a hundred other taunts were hurled with entire freedom at the head of a sturdy boy, to judge from his round and rosy face not more than eleven years old, by six or eight urchins, who were dancing round him with many unfriendly demonstrations. Apparently there had already been an exchange of hostilities. One of the half-dozen had received a blow in the eye which had half closed that organ and another showed signs of having suffered on the nose, much to the damage of his clothing; these injuries had evidently enraged and excited the sufferers. Prudence, however, was not forgotten. They egged each other to the attack, but at the same time showed signs of hesitation, perhaps for want of a leader who might organise a simultaneous rush.

The boy, meanwhile, though he too bore marks of the fray, for his clothes were torn, and a streak of blood on his cheek showed where he had been hit by a stone or a stick, kept a valiant front. He stood with his back against a fine oak, and flourished a short stout cudgel.

"Come on, come on, all of you!" he shouted. "A broken crown the first shall have, I promise you!"

"He's threatening thee, Jack Turner. Hit him over the pate!"

"Look at his jerkin—he's one of the Flemish hogs."

"Flemish!" cried the boy indignantly. "Better English than all of you put together. No English that I know are cowards!"

The dreadfulness of such a charge overcame all fears of broken heads. With a yell of rage the urchins rushed pell-mell upon their foe, and battle, indeed, arose! He defended himself with a courage and vigour worthy of all praise, hitting at weak points, and bestowing at least two of his promised broken heads. But numbers will prevail over the most determined bravery, and here were at least a dozen kicking legs and encumbering arms. Do what he would he could not shake them off, blows rained upon him under which he turned dizzy, and his evil case would soon have been exchanged for a worse, if an unexpected ally had not rushed upon the group. A splendid deer-hound crashed in upon them, upsetting two or three of the boys, though more as if he were amusing himself with a rough frolic than with thought of harm. The urchins, however, did not stay to consider this, for, picking themselves up with cries of terror, they fled as fast as their legs could carry them, leaving sundry spoils behind them in the shape of apples and a spice-cake, which latter the dog, doubtless considering himself entitled to his share of the booty, gobbled up without a moment's hesitation.

The boy who had been the object of attack was the only one who showed no sign of fear. He stood, breathless and panting, his cheeks crimson, his clothes torn, but with so resolute a determination in his face as proved that he was ready for another fight. Seeing, however, that the hound had no ill intentions, he straightened and shook himself, picked up the cap which had fallen off in the fray, and looked round to see who was near.

He saw for the first time that two persons were watching him with some amusement. One was a boy of about fourteen, the other an elderly man in the grey dress of a Franciscan friar.

"Thou art a sturdy little varlet," said the friar, coming forward with a smile, "and held thine own right well. But I doubt me how it would have gone, had Wolf not borne in to the rescue. No shame to thee either, for thou wast sorely overmatched. What had brought such a force of rascaille upon thee?"

The boy had grown rather redder, if that were possible, but he spoke out bravely.

"Holy friar, they were angry because this morning I saved a monkey out of their hands. Its master, an Italian, had died, and they called the poor beast a devil's imp, and were going to stone it to death."

"I would Wolf had served them worse! But why did they not fight with thee at the time?"

"They were but three then," said the boy with a laugh.

"Hum. And who are the little varlets? Give me their names, and they shall have a goodly thrashing."

The boy for the first time hung his head. The other lad, who had been listening impatiently, broke in in French.

"Set Wolf at them in another sort of fashion. I see them still skulking about, and peeping at us from behind the trees—the unmannerly loons! They need to be taught a lesson."

"Gently, Edgar," said the friar, laying his hand on his young companion's arm, "Wolf might prove a somewhat dangerous chastiser. Come, boy, let us have their names," he added, turning to the other.

"Holy friar," said the boy eagerly, "I know the French."

The friar lifted his eyebrows.

"I thought thy tongue had a strange trick about it, but I could have sworn it was Flemish that it resembled."

"We have just come from Flanders."

"Not English," cried Edgar angrily. "If I had known he was one of those blood-sucking foreigners, who fasten like leeches upon our poor country, Wolf should never have bestirred himself to the rescue."

"Peace," said the friar more sharply, but before he could say more the younger boy broke in indignantly—

"We are English, good English! My father has but been in Flanders perfecting himself in his trade of wood-carving."

"And 'twas there you learnt the French?"

"Ay, sir, from the monks."

"Perhaps also thou hast learnt to read?" pursued the friar, with the smile with which in these days we might ask a ploughboy whether he knew Hebrew.

"A little," said the boy modestly.

So unexpected was the answer, that the friar started back.

"Why this is amazing!" he said. "Edgar, dost thou hear?"

"Ay. He is training, no doubt, for the monastery," said the lad carelessly, though looking at the other with amazement.

"Nay," said the boy sturdily; "no monk's hood for me. I would be a soldier and fight for King Edward."

"And what knowest thou of King Edward?" inquired the friar, who evidently found amusement in questioning.

"What all the world knows," the boy answered sturdily, "that never was a nobler king or truer Englishman."

"Ay? Learnt you that in Flanders?" said the friar, lifting his eyebrows in some astonishment. "Well, wherever you had it, 'tis good teaching and true, such as men by-and-by will look back and own. And so nothing will serve thee but hard blows? What is thy name?"

"Hugh Bassett, holy friar."

"Come to the great Stourbridge fair with thy father and mother?"

"My mother is dead. My father has brought some of his carvings here to sell, and we lodge in the sacristan's house because 'tis too cold in the fields."

Wolf, at a call from the young lad, had come back from an investigation among the oaks, and was now slobbering affectionately over his young master's hand; Hugh watching him with deepest interest.

"There is one thing thou hast all but forgotten," said the friar; "the names of thy tormentors? See, they are still watching and peeping."

The boy again hung his head.

"What now? Hast lost thy tongue?"

"Nay, father, but—"

"But what?" Then as Hugh muttered something, "What, I am not to know? Yet they were for serving thee badly enough!"

"I would fight them again," said the boy, looking up boldly.

"I warrant thou wouldst," said the friar, laughing heartily. "And without a mother, who will mend thy clothes? They have suffered more damage than thy tough head, which looks as if 'twere made to bear blows."

Hugh glanced with some dismay at his torn jerkin. It was not the first time that the question had presented itself, though the friar's questions had driven it out of his head. And the elder lad now showed symptoms of impatience.

"May we not be going back, sir?" he said to his companion. "The jongleurs were to be at their play by now, and we are not like to see much out in this green tangle."

"As thou wilt," said the good-tempered friar; "I will but make one more proffer to our valiant friend. See here, Hugh, I have a fancy to know the name of the biggest of thine enemies, the one who set the others on thee. Will a groat buy the knowledge? There it is before thine eyes, true English coin, and no base counterfeit pollard. Only the name, and it is thine."

"Not I!" cried the boy. "I'll have nothing to do with getting him flogged."

"Yet I'll answer for it thy pocket does not see many groats, and what brave things there be to be bought at the fair! Sweets and comfits and spices."

"They would choke me!"

The friar laughed long, with a fat, noiseless chuckle full of merriment.

"Well," he said, "I keep my groat, and thou thine honour, and I see that Wolf hath shown himself, as ever, a dog of discretion. Shall we take the boy back to thy father's lodgings, Edgar, and persuade Mistress Judith to bestow some of her fair mending upon his garments?"

"So as we waste no more time here, I care not," said the lad impatiently.

Bidding the boy follow, Friar Nicholas and his companion walked away, leaving the wood with its undergrowth of bracken, already looking rather brown and ragged with the past heat of the summer, and first touch of frost sharpening the nights in the low-lying Eastern counties, as is often the case by Michaelmas. At that time, towards the end of the thirteenth century, it need hardly be said that the country presented a very different appearance from that which we see now. Parts were densely wooded, and everywhere trees made a large feature in the landscape, which was little broken by human habitations. The chief clearings were effected in order to provide sheep walks, wool being at that time a large, if not the largest, export; although matters had not as yet arrived at the condition of some fifty years later, when, after England was devastated by the Black Death, and agricultural labour became ruinously dear, serfs were evicted from their huts, and even towns destroyed, in order to gain pasturage for sheep. Under Edward the First things were tending the other way; marshes were drained, waste land was brought into cultivation, and towns were increasing in size and importance. Wheat was dear, animal food cheap. Some of the greater barons lived in almost royal state, but the smaller gentry in a simplicity which in these days would be considered absolute hardship.

With an absence of shops, and with markets bringing in no more than the local produce of a few miles round, it will be easily understood how fairs became a need of the times. They began by people flocking to some Church festival, camping out round the church, and requiring a supply of provisions. The town guilds, setting themselves to supply this want, found here such an opening for trade that the yearly fairs became the chief centres of commerce, and had a complete code of laws and regulations. Privileges were even granted to attract comers, for at a fair no arrest could be made for debts, saving such as were contracted at the fair itself. And it was a fruitful source of revenue, because upon everything bought a small toll was paid by the buyer.

Gradually these fairs increased in importance. English traders travelled to those across the seas, to Leipsic, to Frankfort, even to Russia. Foreigners in their turn brought their wares to England, where the principal yearly fair was held at Stourbridge, near Cambridge, another of scarcely less importance at Bristol, and somewhat lesser ones at Exeter and other towns.

The scene at these fairs, when the weather was favourable, was one of extreme gaiety and stir. As the friar and his young companion, followed by Hugh, walked back towards the town a soft autumnal sun was shining on the fields, where were all sorts of quaint and fantastic erections, and where the business of the fair was at its height. Such people as could find house-room were lodged in the town, but these only bore a moderate proportion to the entire throng, and the less fortunate or poorer ones were forced to be content with tents, rude sheds, and even slighter protection. These formed the background, or were tacked on to the booths on which the varied collection of wares were set forth, and which with their bright colourings gave the whole that gay effect which we now only see in the markets of the more mediaeval of foreign towns. To this must be added a large number of motley costumes: here not only were seen the different orders of English life—the great baron with his wife and children, his retinue, squires, men-at-arms, pages; the abbot riding in little less state; friars, grey, black, and white; pilgrims—but foreigners, men of Flanders with richly dyed woollen stuffs, woven from English wool; merchants from the Hans towns displaying costly furs; eastern vendors of frankincense, and spices, and sugar; Lombard usurers; even the Chinaman from Cathay, as China was then called, with his stores of delicate porcelain—each and all calling attention to their wares, and inviting the passers-by, whether nobles or churls, to buy.

The fair originated in a grant to the hospital of lepers at Cambridge, bestowed by King John. It opened on the nineteenth of September, continued for two or three weeks, and was under the control of the master of the leper-house, no slight undertaking when the great concourse of people is considered, for not only had they to be housed and fed, but at a time when carriages and carts were unknown, and men and merchandise were alike carried on horses and mules, there must necessarily have been a vast number of beasts to keep. Protection had to be afforded against possible attacks of robbers or outlaws, and—almost the most difficult task of all—it was necessary to check as far as possible quarrels which frequently arose between the haughty barons or their retainers, as also to protect the foreigners from the rough treatment which it was not unlikely they would receive should anything excite the people against them. Particularly, and it must be owned justly, was this at times the case with the usurers.

But though the nominal business of the fair consisted in trading, money-getting, and money-lending, there were plenty of shows and amusements to attract those who loved laughter. In one part a number of lads were throwing the bar, in another they were playing at what seemed a rough kind of tennis. Merry Andrews tumbled on the green, rope dancers performed prodigies of activity; here men played at single-stick, wrestled, or shot at a mark; at another place were the jongleurs or conjurers, and in yet another a bespangled company of dancing dogs, which excited the lordly contempt of Wolf.

"These fellows have rare skill," said Edgar, watching a conjurer effect a neat multiplication of balls.

"Stay and watch them," said the friar. "Thy father will not yet have ridden back from Cambridge, and thou art not wanted in the house. I will go and do my best to gain Mistress Judith's good aid for this urchin, and after that, if he will, he may show me where he lodges."

Sir Thomas de Trafford, knight of the shire, and father of the lad Edgar, had found accommodation for his family in a house which we should now consider very inadequate for such a purpose, though it was then held to have made a considerable stride towards absolute luxury from being able to boast a small parlour, or talking room. Neither glass nor chimneys, however, were yet in use, although the latter were not unknown, and had crept into some of the greater castles. Fires were made in the centre of the rooms, and the pungent wood smoke made its escape as best it could through door or windows, which in rough weather or at night were protected by a lattice of laths.

The friar, however, went no further than the passage, where he called for Mistress Judith, and was presently answered in person by a somewhat crabbed-looking personage, who listened sourly to his entreaty that she would do something towards stitching together Hugh's unfortunate jerkin.

"The poor varlet has no mother," he ended. But Mistress Judith pursed her mouth.

"The more need he should be careful of his clothing," she was beginning, when suddenly with a rush two little golden-haired girls of not more than four or five came running along the passage, calling joyfully upon Friar Nicholas, and clinging to his grey cloak.

"Thou wilt take us to the fair, wilt thou not?"

"And let us see the monkey that runs up the ladder, and the dancing bear, and—we have some nuts for the monkey."

Mistress Judith's face relaxed.

"Nay, now, children, ye must not be troublesome. The good friar has doubtless other business on hand—"

"I'll take them, I'll take them," said the friar, hastily, "if you will put the boy in order by a few touches of your skilful handiwork. As soon as I have bestowed him in safety I will return for them."

"To see the monkey," persisted little Eleanor.

"Ay, if thou wilt—" He was interrupted by a pull of the sleeve from Hugh.

"So please you, holy friar," said the boy shyly, "the monkey is at our lodging."

"What, is that the poor beast which those young villains would have stoned? Nay, then, hearken, little maidens. The monkey has been in evil case, and was like to be in worse but for this boy, Hugh Bassett. And the cruel varlets who would have killed it set upon him for delivering it, and though he fought right sturdily he would have been in evil case but for Wolf."

"Our Wolf?"

"Even so. What say you now?"

"He is a good boy," said the little Anne gravely. Eleanor went nearer, and looked steadfastly at Hugh.

"Is the poor monkey at your house?"

"Ay, little mistress."

"Shall we come and see him?"

Hugh looked uncertainly at the friar, and the friar at Mistress Judith. Mistress Judith threaded her needle afresh.

"If my lady—" began the friar.

"My lady does not permit my young mistresses to run about the fair like churls' children," interrupted the nurse sourly. "Marry, come up! I marvel your reverence should have thought of such a thing."

She was interrupted in her turn. Eleanor had clambered on a chair and flung her arms round her neck, laying hold of her chin and turning it so as to look in her face, and press her rosy lips to her cheek.

"Nay, nay, mother said we should see the monkey! Thou wilt come with us, and Friar Nicholas, and this good boy. Say yea, say yea, good nurse!"

Mistress Judith, rock with all others, was but soft clay in the hands of her nurslings. She remonstrated feebly, it is true, but Eleanor had her way, and it was not long before the little party set forth, the children indulging in many skips and jumps, and chattering freely in their graceful *langue de Provence*.

There was so much to see, and so many remarks to be made on many things, such wonderful and undreamt of crowds, such enchanting goods, such popinjays, such booths of cakes, such possibilities of spending a silver penny, that it seemed as if the sacristan's house would never be reached, and 'twas easy to see it cost the children something to turn from the fair towards the church. Perhaps Anne would have consented to put their object aside and remain in this busy scene of enchantment. But nothing to Eleanor could balance her desire to see the monkey, and they went their way with no further misadventure than arose from the bag of nuts slipping from her little fingers, and the nuts scattering in all directions.

The sacristan's house consisted of but one room, with the fire as usual in the centre. The sacristan himself was in the church; over the fire sat a thin pale-faced man, engaged in putting the last strokes to a carved oaken box of most delicate workmanship. The monkey, which had been sitting with him, directly the little party appeared, uttered a cry of fear, sprang on the high back of a bench, and from thence to the uncovered rafters of the roof, where it sat jabbering indignantly, and glancing at the visitors with its bright eyes.

The man, who was Stephen Bassett, Hugh's father, rose and greeted them respectfully, though with some amazement at seeing his boy in unknown company.

"Welcome, holy friar," he said. "If you seek John the sacristan, Hugh shall run and fetch him from the church."

"Nay," said the friar, with his easy smile, "I fear me we are on a lighter quest. These little maidens had a longing to behold the monkey, and thy boy offered to bring them here for that purpose." Mistress Judith looked unutterable disgust at the poor room and her surroundings, though she condescended to sit down on a rough stool, from which she first blew the dust. The friar entered into conversation with Stephen Bassett, and the little golden-haired girls pressed up to Hugh.

"Make him come down," said Eleanor pointing.

"He is frightened—I know not," said Hugh, shaking his head. He was, however, almost as anxious as the other children could be to show off his new possession, and, thanks either to an offered nut, or to the trust which the monkey instinctively felt towards his deliverer, the little creature came swiftly down, hanging by hand and tail from the rafters, to intensest delight of both Anne and Eleanor, and finally leaping upon Hugh's shoulder, where it cracked its nut with all the confidence possible. It was small and rather pretty, and it wore much such a little coat as monkeys wear now. Eleanor could not contain her delight. She wanted to have it in her own arms, but her first attempt to remove it from its perch brought such a storm of angry chattering that Anne in terror plucked her sister's little gown and implored her to come away. Eleanor drew back unwillingly.

"Why doesn't he like me?" she demanded. "I love him. What is his name?"

"Agrippa."

"Agrippa! And can he do tricks? Yesterday he did tricks."

"He knows me not yet, mistress," explained Hugh. "His master died suddenly, and he had no other friend."

"But thou wilt be his friend," said Eleanor, looking earnestly at the boy, "and so will I. I will leave him all these nuts. Anne, I would my father would give us a monkey!"

"I like him not," said Anne, fearfully withdrawing yet closer to Mistress Judith. Eleanor knew no fear. She would have taken the little creature in her arms, regardless of its sharp teeth, or of the waiting woman's remonstrances, but that Hugh would not suffer her to make the attempt. He looked at the two little girls with an eager pride and admiration, felt as if he were responsible for all that happened, and had he been twice his age could not have treated them with more careful respect.

Chapter Two.

Stolen Away.

Meanwhile the friar and Stephen Bassett conversed together, seated on a rude bench at the other side of the dimly-lit room. The friar was a man of kindly curiosity, who let his interests run freely after his neighbours' affairs, and, attracted by the boy, whose education had far overpast that of the knight's son, Edgar, he made searching inquiries, which Stephen answered frankly, relating more fully than Hugh how in Flanders, where he had travelled in order to perfect himself in an art not yet brought to a high pitch of excellence in England, his wife had died, and he having been left with the boy on his hands, the child had excited the interest of the monks, who, finding him teachable, had instructed him in the then rare accomplishments of reading and writing.

"He is like to forget them, though," he added with a sigh, "unless in our wanderings we fall upon other brothers as good as those, which is scarce likely."

"Have you thought of his taking the habit?"

"Nay, his bent lies not that way," said Bassett, smiling. The other smiled also.

"Truly, it seemed not so by the lusty manner in which he laid about him but now. And I mind me he spoke of his wish to be a soldier."

"That I will not consent to," Bassett replied hastily; "he shall follow my trade. It would break my heart if I thought that all my labours died with me." He was interrupted by a fit of coughing.

"And where," inquired the Franciscan, "where dost thou purpose going when the fair is ended?"

"In good sooth, holy friar, that is what troubles me. I had thought of London, but I wot not—"

The other leaned forward, resting his elbow on his knee, and his chin in the palm of his hand.

"I wot not either," he said at last, "but in these days there is much noble work akin to thine going on in the great churches and minsters of the kingdom. There is St. Peter's at Exeter, now. One of our order was telling me but lately how gloriously the bishop of that see is bringing it to perfection. The air in those western shires is soft and healing, better for thy cough than London, which has many fens giving out their vapours, to say nothing of the smoke arising from that vile coal the citizens are now trying to burn, and which pours out its choking fumes upon the poor air. Were I thee I would not bestow myself in London."

"Exeter," said Bassett reflectively; "I thank thee for the suggestion. My wife came from those shires, and a bishop with a zeal for decoration might well give me employment."

"The journey is long," put in the friar, with a desire that prudence should have her share in this advice of his which the wood-carver seemed so ready to adopt.

"We are used to journeys and I dread them not."

"Nor fear robbers?"

"I am too poor to tempt them. Besides, our great king has done much for the security of the country, by what I hear. Is it not so, holy friar?"

"Truly it is. But Scotland has taken more of his thought lately, and when the lion is in combat, the smaller beasts slink out to fall on their prey. But if you make your way to Exeter and would go first through London, our house in Newgate Street will give you hospitable lodging.—How now, Mistress Eleanor?"

"It is the monkey, Friar Nicholas—might he not bring it for madam, our mother, to see? He says that Wolf would eat him."

"And in good sooth that were not unlikely. Better be content to come here again and see the little pagan beast, if Mistress Judith does not mislike it. Fare thee well, Master Bassett. I will meet thee again, and hear whether Exeter still has attraction."

Mistress Judith rose and shook her skirts before folding them round her, an operation which the monkey, happening to be close to her on Hugh's shoulder, resented greatly, chattering at and scolding her with all his might. Eleanor screamed with delight, while Anne hid her face; and Hugh, somewhat abashed at Mistress Judith's displeasure, retired with Agrippa to the back of the room, while his father escorted his guests a few paces beyond the door.

He came back and found Hugh enthusiastic over his new friends.

"The dog, father, a noble beast! I would you had seen him! I warrant me Peter the smith's son has had enough of fighting to last him a while. He ran like a deer!"

"And how fell it out?"

Thus questioned a long story had to be told of the ill deeds of Peter, who had been the chief offender; and the damage to Hugh's garments, which Mistress Judith had but hastily caught together, was ruefully exhibited. Stephen shook his head.

"Another time keep thy fighting till a woman is near to back up thy prowess with her needle. Yet—I'll not blame thee. 'Twould have been a cowardly deed to have suffered that poor beast to be stoned. And at least I can mother thee for these bruises and scratches."

He fetched some water as he spoke, took out a few dried herbs from a bag, set them in the water on the fire, and as soon as the decoction was ready bathed the boy's many hurts with a hand as gentle indeed as his mother's could have been. While this was going on he talked to the child with a freedom which showed them to be more than usually companions in the fullest sense of the word.

"What thinkest thou the good friar hit upon? He thought I might find work at one of the great churches which are rising to perfection in the land. And, Hugh, thou hast heard thy mother speak of Exeter? At Exeter there is much of this going on, and if we could get there, I might obtain the freedom of one of the craft guilds, and apprentice thee."

"Ay"—doubtfully.

"Well, why that doleful tone?"

"I would be a soldier, father."

"Serve thy 'prenticeship first and talk of fighting afterwards. Dost thou think King Edward takes little varlets of eleven years old to make his army? Besides—speak not of it, Hugh. My heart is set upon thy carrying on my work. Life has not been sweet for me, and 'tis likely to be short; let me see some fruit before I die."

The boy flung his arms round Bassett's neck.

"Father, talk not like that! I will be what thou wilt!"

"Thou wilt? Promise me, then," said his father eagerly.

"I promise."

Stephen Bassett's breath came short and fast.

"See here, Hugh. Thou art young in years but quick of understanding, and hast been my close companion of late. Thou art ready to engage, as far as thou canst—I would not bind thee too closely," he added, reluctantly—"to renounce those blood-letting dreams of thine, and follow my trade, and, as I well believe thou wilt, make our name famous?"

"Ay," said the little lad gravely, "that will I do. Only—"

"What?"

"If I must needs be cutting something, I would sooner 'twere stone than wood."

"Sayest thou so?" said the carver, rising and walking backwards and forwards in the room. He was evidently disappointed, and was undergoing a struggle with himself. But at last he stopped, and laid his hand kindly upon the boy's shoulder. "As thou wilt, Hugh," he said; "I would not be unreasonable; and truly I believe thy hand finds more delight in that cold unfriendly surface than in the fine responsive grain of the wood. So thou art a carver, choose thine own material. Stone and wood are both needed in the churches. We will go to Exeter. I mind me thy mother had cousins there. We will but wait for the end of the fair, and there will be folk going to London with whom we may journey safely."

The man's sanguine nature as usual overleapt all difficulties. His cough and his breathing were so bad, that others might have well dreaded the effects of a long and toilsome journey, but he would hear of no possible drawbacks, and Hugh was too young to be alarmed, and took the over-bright eyes and occasional flush of the cheek as glad signs that his father was getting well again.

Thanks to Hugh's new friends, moreover, Bassett sold his work, and sold it well. Dame Edith de Trafford sent for him, desiring he would bring his boy and some specimens of his carving. Hugh begged sore to be allowed to take Agrippa, for the joy it would give to the little Eleanor, but his father would not have it. The monkey, though it had attached itself devotedly to Hugh, was capricious with others, variable in temper, and at times a very imp of mischief, and Stephen feared its pranks might offend their new patroness.

Agrippa was, therefore, consigned to the rafters, where he chattered with displeasure at seeing his master go out without him.

"If he is to journey with us, we must get him a cord," said Bassett. "As it is, we shall pass for a party of mountebanks. See that the door is safely closed, for John the sacristan will not be back yet awhile."

The night had been wet, and the gaiety of the fair much bedraggled in consequence. Under foot, indeed, the mud and mire of the trampled grass made so sticky a compound that it was difficult for one foot to follow the other. The poor folk who had been obliged—as numbers were—to sleep on rough boards, raised on four legs from the ground, and but slightly protected from the weather, were in sad plight. Happily the sun had come out, and though there was not much heat in his rays, they served to lessen some of the discomfort, and to bring back a touch of cheerfulness. Peter the smith's son, with one or two others, pointed and grimaced at Hugh as he passed on, without venturing to approach nearer. The goldsmiths were hanging up costly chains and sets of pearls with which to tempt the noble ladies who approached, while a Hans trader called attention to the fact that winter was coming and his furs would protect from cramps and rheumatism. Presently down through the booths rode a party of knights and javelin men, none other than the high sheriff with the four coroners and others, on their way to the shire court, which was to be held that day under the shire-oak a few miles distant. A number of countrymen had already gone off to this meeting, and in a few minutes Hugh saw Wolf bounding along by the side of a smaller group of knights; Edgar was behind with a younger party, and evidently Sir Thomas de Trafford as one of the knights of the shire was proceeding to join the assembly. Many remarks were made by the bystanders, to which Bassett, who had been long out of England, listened attentively. He found that much satisfaction was in general expressed, though one or two malcontents declared that each assembly was but the herald for a demand for money.

"Parliament or no parliament, 'tis ever the same," grumbled one small cobbler, drest in the usual coarse garment reaching just below the knees, and headed by a square cape, too large for his shrunk shoulders: "wars to be waged, and money to be squeezed from our bodies."

"Thine would not furnish the realm with the weight of a silver penny," said a burly countryman, glancing with much contempt at the cobbler. "And when does the king ask for aid except in case of need? If thou hadst, as I friends in Cumberland, I reckon you would be the first to cry out that a stop should be put to these Scotch outlaws harrying the borders."

"And hast thou friends in Gascony, too, Dick-o'-the-Hill?" demanded the little cobbler spitefully.

"Nay, it's been a scurvy trick of the French king, that getting hold of Gascony," put in a baker who had joined the group; "I'm all for fighting for Gascony."

"Well, I'll warrant that our burgesses, Master Dennis and Master Small, will speak their minds against any wicked waste," persisted the cobbler. "'Tis time the king were checked."

"And who has given you burgesses to speak for you, ay, and passed laws putting the ay and the nay into your own hands?" broke in Stephen Bassett indignantly. "I have been out of England for many a long year, but I mind the time, my masters, if you have forgotten, when the parliament was called, not to vote whether or no the money should be raised, but to raise it. Few laws had you in old days, and little voice in them!"

"He speaks the truth," said a grave franklin standing by.

"When, since the days of Alfred, has there been an English king like our King Edward?" added Dick-o'-the-Hill.

"One that ever keeps his word."

"And makes laws for the poor."

"I say that none speak against him except traitors and false loons," said the baker, squaring up towards the cobbler in a threatening manner.

"Nay, my masters, I meant no harm," urged the cobbler, alarmed. "The saints forbid that I should say a word against King Edward! Doubtless, we shall pay our twelfth, such of us as can—and be as much better as we are like to be."

He added these words under his breath, but Stephen Bassett caught them.

"Ay," he said, "so long as we are saved from sinking into a nation of curs such as thee."

The cobbler cast an infuriated look at him as he walked on, the flush which Hugh loved to see on his cheek.

"That was an evil man, father," said the boy. Bassett was silent for a space.

"There are many such discontented knaves," he returned at last, "eating like a canker into the very heart of our nation. Self, self, that is the limit to which their thoughts rise. And they measure all others by their own petty standard—even the king. It makes one sick at heart to think what he has done for his country, and how—to hear some of these mean-spirited loons talk—it is turned against him, and besmirched, till fairest deeds are made to look black, and nothing is left to him but his faults."

If Hugh could not understand all, he took in much, and remembered it afterwards. But the delights of the fair drove all else out of his head for the moment, and he could scarce be torn away from the dancing bear.

"Hearken," said his father at last with a laugh, "whatever happens, I'll have none of the bear! His masters may die, and he be baited by all the dogs in the town, but he shall never be my travelling fellow. Come, 'tis time we were at the lady's."

This time they were passed through the passage to the talking room, where Dame Edith was sitting on a bench or low settle. The walls were unplastered, its rough floor uncarpeted, its windows unglazed, to modern notions it would have seemed little better than a cell, but Dame Edith herself created about her an air of refinement and delicacy. After the new fashion, instead of the plaits which had been worn, her fair hair was turned up and enclosed in a network caul of gold thread, over which was placed a veil. She wore a kirtle of pale blue silk, and a fawn-coloured velvet mantle, with an extravagantly long train embroidered in blue. She looked too young to be the mother of Edgar, and indeed was Sir Thomas's second wife, and the very darling of his heart. The twins, especially Anne, strongly resembled her; Eleanor had more of her father's and her step-brother's eager impetuosity, but Anne bade fair to be as sweet-mannered and dainty as her mother. Bassett and his son had hardly made their greeting, before the little maidens were in the room, Eleanor so brimming over with questions about the monkey that she could scarce keep her tongue in check.

Dame Edith smiled very kindly on the boy.

"I have heard all the tale from Friar Nicholas," she said, "and of how discreetly Wolf came to the rescue. And so thou wouldst be a soldier?"

Hugh coloured, and his father broke in—

"Nay, lady, he hath laid by that foolish fancy. He will be a carver, like myself."

She lifted her pretty eyebrows.

"In good sooth? Now we had settled matters quite otherwise. I had won my good husband to consenting that he should be taken into our meiné, and there he might have risen. Is the subject quite decided?"

"Quite, lady," Bassett said firmly. "I thank you very humbly for your goodness, but Hugh and I must hold together while I live, and I have set my heart upon his carving a name for himself with a lowlier but a more lasting weapon than the sword."

His cough shook him again as he spoke, and Dame Edith, though unused to opposition, was too kindly natured to show displeasure. She asked to see what he had brought, and was soon wrapt in admiration at the free and delicate work which was displayed. Meanwhile, Eleanor could whisper to Hugh—

"Hath Agrippa eaten all the nuts? Doth he like spice-bread or figs? I'll give thee some. But oh, I wish, I wish thou hadst brought him! Wolf is gone to the shire-oak. And see now, bend down thy head, and hearken to a secret. Madam, our mother, has a silken cord for thee to hold him with. When may we come again and see him? I should like it to be to-day."

Dame Edith was a liberal purchaser. Her last choice was a beautiful little reliquary box, minutely carved, yet with a freedom of design which enchanted her. She would scarcely allow them to leave her, and the afternoon had advanced before father and son found themselves on their way back to the sacristan's house. He met them at the door— a little, withered old man—in an indignant temper.

"Folk should shut the door behind them, and not leave the house to be pillaged," he said, crossly. "Here I come back and find all in disorder, and the door wide open to invite all the ill loons in the place to come in and work their will."

"We left the door safely shut," said Bassett, in surprise.

"Father—Agrippa!" cried Hugh, bolting into the house.

His fears were too true. No Agrippa chattered his welcome to them from the rafters, and as he always remained in that place of refuge during their absence, and was too timid to come down to any stranger, it was evident that some dire abduction had taken place. Hugh, who had grown very fond of the monkey, was like one distracted. John, the sacristan, who loved it less, was disposed to be philosophical.

"Well, well, well," he said, "if the varlets have taken nought else I wish them joy of their bargain, and 'tis well it's no worse. By 'r Lady, 'tis a foul thing to break into a man's house, and we shall see what the Master of the College will say to the watch."

"I'll find the poor beast, if he be still alive," said Hugh, with a choke in his voice, "wherever they've bestowed him. 'Tis Peter's work!"

He was rushing out when Bassett checked him.

"Softly, softly," he said, "prudence may do more than valour in this case. Let us ask a few questions to begin with. Master John, at what time came you back?"

"At four o' the clock, and found the door open—thus, and the tankard of ale I had left emptied. The scurvy knaves! But there's no virtue left in the watch since Master Simpkins got the upper hand, and hath upset all the ancient customs."

Scarce restraining Hugh's impatience, his father made inquiries at some of the houses round, and ended at last in gaining information. Goody Jones was sick of a fever, and her little grandchild, playing at bob-apple before the door with another, had seen Peter, the smith's son, and two other boys, whom she named, go into the sacristan's house. Pressed to say whether she saw them come out again, she said nay. Her grandam had called her, and she had run in.

Link the first was therefore established.

Hugh was for rushing at once to Peter, and forcing the rest out of him, but Bassett counselled more wary walking.

"'Tis a deep-laid plot," he said, "and it were best to meet craft by craft. Besides, if they are accused, they may kill the poor beast to save themselves and spite thee. Let us go out to the fair, and maybe we shall pick up some tidings."

It was dreadful to Hugh to behold Peter in the distance, and to be restrained from falling upon him, and the fair had quite lost its charm, though the noise and stir had increased. Costard-mongers were bawling apples—red, white, and grey costards—at the top of their voices; pig-women inviting the passers-by to partake of the roast pig which smoked on their tables; tooth-drawers and barbers, each proclaiming his calling more loudly than the other. The abbot of a neighbouring monastery had his palfrey surrounded by a group of clothiers, while a fool in motley was the centre of another group. Among these the wood-carver spied a sturdy yeoman, the same Dick-o'-the-Hill who had opposed the cobbler earlier in the day. It struck him that here was a man for his purpose, and he managed to extract him from the others, and to tell him what they were seeking. Honest Dick-o'-the-Hill scratched his head.

"If you knew where they had disposed the beast," he said, "and breaking of heads could do it, I'm your man. But as for finding where 'tis hid, my wife would tell you I was the veriest numskull!" The next moment he brightened. "I have it! There's my cousin before us, carrying that fardel of hay. He's the wisest head for miles round, and I'll warrant he'll clap some sense on the matter. Hi, Mat! Ancient Mat!"

Thus adjured, a small, dried-up, pippin-faced man paused on his way, and waited till his cousin overtook him and explained what was amiss. He listened testily, showing profound contempt for honest Dick's straightforward, though somewhat heavy-handed, suggestions, but more deference towards Stephen Bassett.

"More likely that the knaves have sold than harmed the creature," he pronounced at the end of the story.

"Find out where it is, and I'll do what cracking of crowns is needed," said Dick.

"Mend thine own, which is cracked past recovery," growled the other. "Hearken, master,"—to Bassett—"who is likely to buy such a beast?"

"Some noble household."

"Rather some puppet-show or party of mountebanks; those who have dancing dogs or a bear."

"Right!" cried Stephen, joyfully. "What a fool was I not to think of it!"

"I said he had the best head in the shire," said Dick, with triumph.

"And," continued Matthew, unheeding, "thou wottest that the licence to all foreigners expires to-day, and that they must leave the fair? See there, those Flemish traders are putting their wares together, and the abbot has made a good bargain for his silken hangings. My counsel is to go to the watch, and, when the bear and his masters are on the march, search for the monkey. If I mistake not they will not be able to hide him."

"Well thought of, friend," said Bassett, heartily. "No need of the watch, though," put in Dick-o'-the-Hill; "I'll bring a stout fellow or two who'll do what is necessary."

"Ay, and get us trounced up as the trailbastons the king hates, numskull," said his cousin. "But 'tis nothing to me. Go thine own way for an obstinate loggerhead!"

Dick, who seemed to regard Mat's railing as something rather honourable than otherwise entered into the proposal with extreme zest. He produced a quarterstaff, which he flourished with formidable ease, declaring himself ready with its aid to encounter the bear himself. Stephen Bassett hoped to carry the matter through peaceably, but he felt that his efforts might go more smoothly backed up by a display of force, and welcomed Dick's assistance, as well as that of a neighbour whom he offered to fetch. There was not much time to lose, and they agreed to meet at a certain spot within half an hour, a time which to Hugh's impatience seemed interminable. His father had enough to do in keeping him quiet, and in finding out where the watch, whose business it was to keep order at the fair, were bestowed. Matthew, having disposed of his hay, rejoined Bassett, really desirous to know whether his surmises turned out to be correct; but, as he declared, solely that he might help to check his cousin Dick's ignorant zeal.

Four of them, therefore, to say nothing of Hugh, took up their position in the field just on the outskirts of the fair, and waited patiently or impatiently, after their natures, for the event.

Soon a motley crowd began to emerge from the booths. The most picturesque features of the show, indeed, were departing, for foreigners were not allowed to compete with the English traders beyond a certain number of days; and Flemish, Italians, Chinese, streamed forth, to find a night's lodging as best they might beyond the forbidden limits. This expulsion was accompanied by a good deal of coarse jesting and railing from the other sellers, who rejoiced at the departure.

It was not long before the bear appeared, led by two men.

"Father, father!" cried Hugh, in a tumult of excitement.

"Speak the word, master, when thou desirest an appeal to my quarterstaff," put in Dick-o'-the-Hill, "or even give me a nod, and I'll warrant I'll not be backward. I'll answer for the bear."

"Ay, I verily believe thy head to be as thick as its own," said Matthew. "When wilt thou learn that brains are better than fists? Peace, and keep back."

Stephen Bassett had stepped out, and civilly informed the men that a monkey had been taken from his house, and that he had reason to think it might be in their possession.

"Going beyond known facts," muttered Matthew, "yet one must sometimes make a leap in the dark. They shake their heads and deny. What next? Friend Stephen presses his demand, and all four knaves wax violent in vowing lies; and Dick is puffing and blowing with desire to break heads. They have the beast, but where?"

His quick eyes, darting hither and thither, had soon answered this question. One or two of the men had bundles on their backs, and a boy carried something of the same sort, though smaller. Matthew noticed that, at a word from one of the men, this boy slipped out of the group, and, avoiding the side where Dick and his neighbour Hob were mounting guard, passed round near Matthew himself. In an absolutely unexpected moment he found himself caught by the arm, and though he fought and kicked he was held in a vice. The men turned upon Matthew with threatening gestures, and Dick, in high delight, flourished his quarterstaff, and pressed up to the defence with one eye on the bear, who in a free fight might be held to represent an unknown quantity.

Finding they had fallen into powerful hands the Italians confined themselves to pouring out violent ejaculations, while Hugh flung himself upon the bundle. His fingers trembled so much with excitement that he could hardly drag out the wooden skewers which served to keep it together, but in a minute or two it was unrolled, and the terrified monkey sprang out. He had made one frightened leap already when Hugh's call checked him, and the next moment, with a cry of delight, almost human in its intensity, he ran to the boy, and clambering on his shoulder gave the most unmistakable signs of pleasure.

"The monkey is his own jury," said Matthew, sententiously. "Tried and found guilty, my masters."

The Italians, however, had no intention of giving up their booty without a struggle, and they called upon several jongleurs, who had crowded round, to assist them. One went so far as to seize the monkey, whereupon Dick's cudgel, describing a circle in the air, came down upon the head of the assailant with such force that he dropped like a stone, and Hob following up with another blow scarcely less formidable, it seemed likely that here would be a battle royal. Two men fell upon Matthew, who would have been in evil case had not Dick done as much for him as he had for the monkey; and Stephen

Bassett was set upon with a vigour which soon left him breathless, although Hugh, clasping Agrippa with one hand, with the other arm laid about him to such excellent purpose that he hoped to save his father from hurt till Dick could come to the rescue.

But might has been often found to get the upper hand of right, and both Stephen and Dick had fallen into the common English error of underrating their opponents. A good many of the foreigners had closed round with the desire to help their own body, and without knowing anything of the quarrel; and the English, who would have stoutly taken the opposite side, could only see that some quarrel was going on, and supposed the strangers to be fighting among themselves. Dick had done prodigies of valour, and dealt furious blows with his quarterstaff, but he was hampered by numbers who clung to his arm, and by the charge of protecting his cousin, and he was reluctantly framing a call for rescue when a party of horsemen rode into the very thick of the struggling mass, and scattered it in all directions.

Chapter Three.

Rescued.

It was time. Stephen Bassett was all but spent, and Hugh, trying his best to shield him, was pressed backwards until, to his terror, he found himself close to the hairy form of the bear. But the instant the knights appeared the throng opened and fled, except the bear-leaders, who, hampered by their unwieldy animal, prepared to put the best face they could on the matter.

For the first few minutes, indeed, there was nothing but trying to quiet the horses, frightened out of their senses by finding themselves in close neighbourhood with the bear, and this gave time for Hugh to look, and to cry out joyfully—

"Father, it is Sir Thomas de Trafford! He will see justice done."

"How now, my masters?" cried the knight, a dark-haired, bright-eyed man with a red face. "What means this brawling?"

"Your worship," said Dick-o'-the-Hill, wiping his face with the back of his hand, "these knaves have been taken in the very act of stealing."

"Is that you, Dick Simpkins?" said Sir Thomas, with a laugh. "I might have guessed that heads could not be broken without your having a hand in the breaking. But the King will have none of this violence, and the Master of the Hospital will have thee up for it, neck and crop."

Dick, looking somewhat sheep-faced at this view of his conduct, was yet going to reply, when his cousin Matthew pushed forward.

"Hearken not to him, your worship," he began; "he is an ignorant though a well-meaning knave. But I humbly bid your worship take notice that these men be the culprits who have stolen our property, and, when we would have reclaimed it, set upon us, and were like to have killed us."

"Killed us forsooth!" muttered Dick, stirred to anger at last.

"—Had your worship not come to our rescue. And as witness, knowing all the circumstances—none better—I claim, if they are put upon their trial, to take my place as one of the twelve jurors. It is a case of flagrant delict."

The culprits, conscious of their guilt, but not understanding the conversation, stood as pale as death, glancing from one to the other.

"Let us hear in plain words what hath been stolen," said Sir Thomas, impatiently.

"Please your worship," said Hugh, stepping forward and holding out the monkey, "it is Agrippa."

"A monkey! Why, thou must be the urchin my little maidens are for ever chattering about. And Edgar—where is Edgar? Not here? The youngster is stopping in the fair. And did these fellows steal thy monkey?"

Bassett, who had recovered his breath, put in his word.

"Ay, your worship; when we were away at your lady's, showing her the carved work of mine she would see. We left the door of John the sacristan's—where we are lodging—shut, and came back to find it open and the monkey gone."

"Might he not have escaped?"

"He was too timid unless he had been driven forth. Besides, we have evidence that the boy, who hath shown much ill-will already in the matter, was seen to go in at the door with two others. If these men are questioned I believe they will tell us that they bought the beast from these boys, and your worship may hold their fault the less."

The knight growled something in his beard which was not flattering to foreign traders; but his sense of justice led him to take the course which Bassett suggested, and he put his questions in French to the Italians, who, watching the faces of those around (of whom a considerable number had now collected), were in mortal terror of short shrift. By all the saints in the calendar they vowed that no thought of stealing had crossed their minds. A boy had brought the monkey; they could understand no more than that he wanted to sell it, and, as they were glad of the opportunity, they gave him ten silver pennies for their bargain.

Matthew was greatly vexed not to understand this defence, in which he would have been ready enough to pick holes; but Bassett, knowing that, though true in the main, their story said nothing to explain their denial of having seen the monkey or of its concealment in the bag, kept merciful silence. The men, at any rate, had been punished by fright, and when Sir Thomas de Trafford asked if he demanded that they should be haled back and given over to the college authorities he shook his head.

"E'en let them go, so we have the monkey," he said.

The knight administered a sharp rating, and bade them tie up their comrade's broken head and be off; a permission of which they were only too glad to avail themselves, the bear shuffling after them and causing a fresh panic among the horses.

"Quiet, Saladin!" said Sir Thomas, irritably. "Master Carver, somebody must suffer for this, and the boy who stole and sold the beast is the worst offender. Thou—what is thy name—Hugo? Hugh?—what sayest thou should be done to him?"

"Your worship," said Hugh, tingling all over with eager thrill of hope, "your worship, I should like to fight him."

"Trial by combat," said the knight, laughing.

"Nay, nay, he's a false loon, and that were too honourable a punishment. Here, Dick-o'-the-Hill, thou knowest every knave for miles round, go to the watch, and bid them take the thievish young varlet to the whipping-post, and let him remember it. Tell them I will answer for them to their masters."

"Tell them," Matthew called after him, "that it is a case of flagrant delict."

"Here, Master Carver," said Sir Thomas, moving his horse a few paces off and beckoning to Bassett, "that boy of thine is a gallant little urchin, and my babies have taken a fancy to him. Wilt thou spare him to us? He shall be well eared for; my lady has but too soft a heart, as I tell her, for the youngsters of the household."

"I am deeply beholden to your worship," returned Stephen, hastily. "It sounds ungracious to refuse so good an offer, but I cannot part with him while I live. You may guess from my face that that will not be for long."

At the first part of this speech Sir Thomas had frowned heavily, but he could not be wroth with the end.

"The more reason," he said, "that the boy should have a protector."

"True," Bassett answered. "I have thought much of that. But I hope to have time yet to place him somewhere where he can follow my craft and build his own fortunes."

"And you would throw away his advancement for a dream?"

"Is it a dream?" said the carver. "Believe me, your worship, that, although you may find it hard to believe, we men of art have our ambitions as strong in us as in the proudest knight of King Edward's court. Hugh has that in him which I have fostered and cherished, and which I believe will bear fruit hereafter and bring him, or his art, fame."

"Small profits, I fear me," said Sir Thomas.

"That is like enough. It may be not even a name. But something will he have done, as I believe, for the glory of God and the honour of his art."

"Well," said the knight, half vexed, "I have made thee a fair offer, and the rest lies with thyself. Where go you after the fair?"

"By Friar Nicholas's advice, gentle sir, as far as to Exeter. He thinks I may meet with work there and a softer air."

"Since thy father will have nought better, I must find a gift for thee, boy," said the knight, reining back his horse. He drew a richly-chased silver whistle from his breast and threw it to the boy. "Take good care of Agrippa; my little Nell would have broken her heart if she had heard he was gone. Good day, friend Matthew; good day, Master Carver."

The next moment the little party had clattered away, leaving Hugh with thanks faltering on his tongue, and Matthew on tip-toe with pride at his own discernment.

"Never would you have seen your monkey again if I had not collared the knave," he said. "Now, there is my cousin Dick, an honest fellow as ever swung a flail, but with no thought beyond what he can do with fists and staff; no use of his eyes, no putting two and two together. I'll warrant me by the time he reaches the watch he will have forgotten the words I put into his mouth; and yet they are the very pith of the matter. I'll e'en go after him."

He started off, while Bassett and his boy made their way back towards the church, Hugh ill at ease because, while the pommelling of Peter seemed a fine thing, his doom to the whipping-post, though no more than justice, gave him an uneasy feeling. But his father would hear of no going to beg him off, and, indeed, it would have been bootless. Peter's offence was one for which whipping might be held a merciful punishment—

"And may save him from turning into a cut-purse later on," added Bassett.

So Agrippa went back to his rafters and met with no more adventures. The fair ran its usual busy course; the friar came often to talk with Stephen Bassett and to give Hugh exercises in reading and writing; while, more rarely, Eleanor and Anne appeared with Mistress Judith—in great excitement the last time because the next day they were to set forth for their home. September was drawing to an end, the weather was rainy, and Bassett began to make inquiries as to parties who would be travelling the same road as himself. Dick-o'-the-Hill was certain that his cousin Mat would find the right people. He had implicit faith in his sagacity, and came with him in triumph one day to announce success. It seemed that a mercer, his wife, and son were going back to London and would be glad of company. And then it came out that Matthew himself was strongly drawn in the same direction.

"A man," he explained, "is like to have all his wits dulled who sees and hears none but clodhoppers. I feel at times as if I were no sharper than Dickon here. Now in London the citizens are well to the front. There is the Alderman-burgh, with the Law Courts and the King's Bench, there is the Lord Mayor, there is the King's Palace at Westminster and the great church of St. Paul's; much for a man of understanding to see and meditate upon, Master Bassett, and I have half a mind—"

"Have a whole one, man," cried the carver, heartily; "and I would Dick would come too."

"Nay, in London I should be no better than an ass between two bundles of hay," said honest Dick, shaking his head. "But if Mat goes he will bring us back a pack of news, and maybe might see the king himself."

It did not take much to give a final push to Matthew's inclination. He had neither wife nor child, and, as he confided to Bassett, his bag of marks would bear a little dipping into. He bought a horse—or rather Dick bought it for him—the carver agreeing to pay him a certain sum for its partial use during their journey to London, and they set out at last, leaving the fair shorn of its glory.

Folk were travelling in all directions; but London was the goal of the greater number, and the little knots of traders with one consent, for fear of cut-purses, kept well within sight of each other. The road was not bad, although a course of wet weather might quickly convert it into a quagmire; and it was easy enough to follow, for one of the king's precautions against footpads was the clearing away of all brushwood and undergrowth for a space of two hundred feet on each side of the highway as well as round the gates of towns. A great deal of talk passed between the different groups, for fairs were the very centre of news, foreign and English, political and commercial, with a strong under-current of local gossip. The Hansards, Easterlings, and Lombards had brought the latest information about the French claims to Gascony, as well as much trading information from Bruges, which was then the great seat of commerce; the English merchants discussed the king's wise and politic measures to promote the unity of the kingdom, a cause which Edward had much at heart, as necessary not only for the greatness but the safety of that England for whose good never king toiled more unselfishly.

It was all deeply interesting to Stephen Bassett, who had left his own country many years before, and was amazed at the strides civil liberties had made since that time. Before this the making and the keeping of laws had depended upon the fancies of the reigning king, checked or enlarged as they might be by the barons. It was Edward the First who called his Commons to assist in the making of these laws, who summoned burgesses from the principal towns throughout the kingdom, who required the consent of the people for Acts proposed in Parliament, and enforced the keeping of these laws so powerfully that his greatest lords could no more break them with impunity than the meanest churl. He set up a fixed standard of weights and measures. Up to this time all attempts in this direction had been failures, and the inconvenience must have been great. He tried to encourage the growth of towns, freeing them from petty local restrictions and introducing staples or fixed markets. Under him taxation became more general and more even. He made a survey of the country yet more important than that of Domesday. And if that honourable hold of plighted word was—at any rate until late years— the proud characteristic of an Englishman, this national virtue, which does not come by chance any more than does a personal virtue, is owing in no small degree to the steady and strong example of the great king, who on his tomb left that bidding to his people—"Pactum serva"—keep covenant.

Hugh, for love of his father, listened as well as he could to the talk; but he had good play-times as well, for there were many boys and girls on the road, and, indeed, the mercer with whom they travelled had his lad of thirteen with him. Agrippa, held by Dame Edith's silken cord, was an immense object of interest; the mercer's wife made him a new little coat of scarlet cloth, and, besides the black rye bread which he shared with his masters, the children were never tired of bringing him nuts, costard apples, and spice-nuts, so that he fared well. He showed great affection for Hugh, and was never so happy as when on his shoulder; tolerating Stephen and detesting Matthew.

The hostels were crowded, and the accommodation of the roughest; but it was always a matter of rejoicing to have got through the day's journey without encounter of outlaws. Highway robbery was one of the evils with which the king had vigorously to contend, and at their last halting-place the host's wife had such a number of terrible stories at her fingers' ends as made the more timorous shake in their shoes. She discoursed volubly as she brought in an excellent supper, which they ate with knives, forks being as yet a great luxury.

"Alack-a-day, my masters!" she said. "I wot that shameful things have happened on this very road not so long ago. My lord Abbot from the neighbouring house, having but one brother with him, was seized and robbed, and left bound in the ditch. The thief made off with his palfrey, and that led to his being taken and hung; but the abbot, holy man! has scarce recovered from the shock."

One story brings another, and Matthew was seldom behindhand when anything had to be said.

"Things be better, however, than they were ten years ago. Then was a time of riot. I mind me I had a cousin, living in Boston, when there came to the gates one night a party of monks wanting room in the monastery. Fine monks were these, for, when all honest citizens were in bed, out they slipped, stripped off their gowns, appeared in doublet and hose of green, and never trust me, my masters, if these merry men did not take the town so completely by surprise that they sacked and set fire to it before they left."

"There, see now!" cried the hostess, lifting up her hands; "and they might do the same by us now, and we sleeping in our beds like babes!"

"I warrant that was what caused the king to ordain that town gates should be closed between sunset and sunrise, and makes him so strict in the matter," said a monk who was seated at table, with a good helping of a fish called cropling on his trencher. "Nay, good mistress, look not mistrustfully on me. I wear no cassock of green, only that which belongs to the habit of St. Austin, of which I am an unworthy brother."

"There be land pirates and sea pirates," said the little red-faced mercer, pompously; "both be enemies to an honest man's trade."

"Alack, I know not how any can venture on the seas!" added his wife, putting her head as much on one side as her stiff gorget would allow.

"There's terrible venturesome folk nowadays," put in the hostess, pouring out a tankard of ale.

"They do say that ships be going so far as Spain; never will they come back again, that's certain." Bassett listened, smiling, to these doleful conjectures; at the same time, hearing more of the dangers of the highways made him think with some anxiety of the long journey to Exeter which lay before them. His strength had been tried by that now going on, and he wished it had been earlier in the year, when the days had been longer and roads better. But he was naturally hopeful, and, comforting himself with the thought that on the next day, if all was well, they would reach London, he listened patiently to much which Hugh had to tell about his comrades on the road and Agrippa's cleverness before stretching themselves on the hard pallet which fell to their share in the common room.

Chapter Four.

God Save the King!

The last day's journey was a heavy one, owing to the rain which fell persistently. All the travellers wore their long pointed hoods, and carried tall, stout sticks, but their legs were not very well protected except by thick hose, and Bassett's cough was none the better for the journey. He was glad enough when they came near the clusters of houses or villages which marked the outskirts of London, and saw the mist hanging over the city which, helped by the moisture from the marshes, the new use of coal was already beginning to produce. Matthew was in a high state of delight.

"Truly something of a city!" he exclaimed, rubbing his hands, "sheltering within its walls something like forty thousand souls. A noble city! I'll warrant a man of parts might make a name here. There are the walls."

The carver was almost too weary to bear Hugh's questionings as to the Franciscan monastery in Newgate Street where they were to lodge, and whether the prior might object to the presence of Agrippa. When they reached the monastery, indeed, he was so sorely spent that the good friars at once called one of their number who had studied physic and consigned Bassett to his care, giving him, moreover, the best room in the guests' quarters.

It must be said that the monkey was very doubtfully received, indeed he might probably have been altogether refused, for some of the brethren looked upon him as an actual imp of Satan, or perhaps Satan himself. But the prior was of a larger nature, so that Hugh was suffered to take Agrippa with him into the room he shared with his father.

And here, in spite of his impatience, Bassett was forced to spend a week, Friar Luke altogether refusing to allow his patient to leave the room until the cough and pain in his side were subdued. Had it not been for his strong longing to reach Exeter and see Hugh started as an apprentice this would have been a time of peace for the carver. His quarters were sunny and cheerful; Friar Luke was a herbalist, and in his search for healing plants would bring him back what autumn flowers yet lingered, and talking of them would draw out stores of simple learning. Agrippa, moreover, somewhat to Friar Luke's discomfiture, had shown a strong attraction for his master's physician, and would come flying down from all manner of unexpected places to greet him. Sometimes the prior would visit his guest, and, being a man of thought, his presence was a real delight to Stephen, while the prior was glad to hear the experiences of a man who had travelled largely and seen something of the world. As Stephen grew stronger Friar Luke allowed him to attend the services in the chapel.

Then Hugh would come in, rosy and excited with his walks with Matthew, who would see everything, even to the hangings on the Tyburn elms. They went to mass at St. Paul's, then surrounded by its own walls; they walked down the grassy spaces of Strand; they looked with some dread at the round church of the New Temple, and heard tales of the Templars fit to make the hair stand on end; they passed another day to the village of Westminster, where was the king's palace and the beautiful abbey, together with the great hall where Parliament, when it met in London, assembled. It amused Hugh very well at first to see the crowds of suitors who poured up the stairs—those who had some complaints to make, grievances to be redressed, or petitions to be laid before the Triers. No hindrance was put in their way; everyone was free to come, each had a fair hearing. Outlaws came to beg for pardon, when, if the Triers thought fit, they were recommended to the king's grace; men and women sought redress from wrongs inflicted perhaps by the lord of the manor; jurors who had perverted their office were brought up to receive judgment—all these lesser matters were as much the business of Parliament as granting aids to the king for carrying on the wars, and so fascinated was Matthew with the scene that Hugh was wearied to death of it before he could drag him away.

He got him out at last, muttering to himself that had he but known how easy matters were made he would have looked up a case of his own against the University of Cambridge. Hugh, stirred by ambition to have to do with an actual suitor, which was much more exciting than looking on and listening to matters he did not understand, was for his going back again at once. Great was Matthew's indignation at the idea.

"Thou silly oaf!" he said, angrily. "To go without preparation!"

"They but told a plain story," returned Hugh, sturdily. "Anyone could do as much."

"Seest thou not the difference? They were ignorant men with whom the Council was wondrous patient, overlooking all their clipped words, and mercifully stooping to their simpleness. But for a man of understanding to put a case matters must be very different. Fit words must he use, and just pleadings must he make, and be ready to give good reason. Their worships know well with whom they have to do. I will take thee to the Guildhall one day, and there thou shalt see the lawyers in their white coifs. They are no longer monks, as once they were."

"I would liefer go down the river and see the ships," said Hugh wearily.

Matthew, who was really good-natured, yielded to this desire, and they picked their way along the swampy ground as best they could, and past the Tower. The great trade of London, even at this time when commerce was ever made secondary to politics, was so large that a number of vessels were in the river. Strange craft they were and of all shapes and sizes, the largest resembling nothing so much as a swollen half-circle, broadening at one end, and coming round so as to form a sort of shelter, and curving sharply to a point at the bow. No such thing as sea charts as yet existed, so that a voyage was a perilous matter, and, in spite of the Crusades and of the trade with the Mediterranean, few vessels ventured through the Straits of Gibraltar. Edward was turning his attention to the navy, and was the first to appoint admirals, but, so far, England's strength lay altogether in her army and her famous bowmen, and the sea was no source of power, nor her sailors famous.

Still, though Matthew professed the greatest contempt for his taste, Hugh found the river more delightful than the Council Hall, and was for lingering there as late as he could. Some of the vessels were unloading, others embarking corn from the eastern counties, so that there was much stir and turmoil, and more vessels were in than was usual, because the time of the autumn equinox was dangerous for sailing. Children, too, were, as ever, playing about, and one group attracted Hugh, because in it was a little maid much about the size of little Eleanor, and with something of her spirited ways. The boys, her companions, were rough, and at last one pushed her with such force that she fell, striking her head violently against a projecting plank. Hugh flew to avenge her, but the boys, frightened at seeing her lie motionless, fled, and Matthew stood growling at the manners of the age. Hugh, used to sickness, ran to the water's brink, and scooped up a little water in his two hands. By the time he had poured it on her face and raised her head on his knee she opened her brown eyes with a cry of "Mother!" and the next moment a man in a sailor's dress had leaped ashore from one of the vessels which were lading close by, had run to the group and taken her in his arms.

"Art thou hurt, my Moll, and where?"

"Father, 'twas Robin Bolton pushed me."

"Ay, and I wot Robin Bolton shall have a clout on his head when he comes within my reach. But there, thou wilt soon be well again. Thank thee for thy help," he added, more roughly, to Hugh.

"If you stand in need of a witness," began Matthew, but the sailor interrupted him—

"Witnesses? No! What she stood in need of was water, which thy boy fetched. He is quick enough to be a sailor," he added, with a laugh.

"Wilt thou come on a voyage to Dartmouth?"

"I should be frighted on the sea," said Hugh sturdily.

"Nay, it's not so bad, so you fall not in with pirates, which are the pest of our coasts. I've been lucky enough to escape them so far. But then," he added with a wink, "they know me at Dartmouth, and folk sometimes tell evil tales of Dartmouth."

He was of a talkative nature, or perhaps thought it well to keep his Moll quiet on his knee, for he went on to tell them that his wife and child lived near the spot where they were, while he went on trading voyages, bringing up Cornish ore from Dartmouth and carrying back other ladings. He was very proud of his vessel, and yet prouder of his little maid, whom it was plain he did his best to spoil; and when he saw that she had taken a fancy to Hugh, he told him he might come on board his vessel one day before he sailed.

"Which will be in a week," he said, confidently. "The storms will be over by then."

Hugh was glad enough of the bidding, for Matthew, with his love for the law courts and for all that concerned the State, was but a dry companion to an eager boy. He went back to the monastery in high glee, to tell his father all that he had heard.

Friar Luke was with Stephen, having brought his patient a decoction of coltsfoot, and also a little bunch of flowers which he was examining with enthusiastic patience.

"See here," he said, with a sigh, "though in good sooth one needs eyes of more than human power to examine so minute a structure. There is a talk that one of our order, Friar Bacon, who died not many years ago, could by means of a strange instrument so enlarge distant objects as to bring them into the range of a man's vision. I know not. Many strange things are told of him, and many of our brethren believe that he had dealings with the black art. It might be he was only in advance of us all. But while he was about it I would he had taught us how to enlarge what is near. And, indeed, there is talk of a magic beryl—"

"Father, father!" cried Hugh, rushing in breathless; "we have been to the river, and there was a ship, and a little maiden called Moll, and the master has bid me on board the ship before he sails for Dartmouth."

He poured out the history of the day, standing by his father's knee, with Agrippa nestling in his arms. Bassett heard him so thoughtfully that Hugh began to think he was displeased.

"Mayn't I go?" he asked, tremulously.

"Ay, ay," said his father, absently. "Friar Luke, tell me truly, do you still dread for me this journey to Exeter?"

"Rather more than less," answered the friar.

"The fatigue?"

"Ay, fatigue and exposure, but chiefly the fatigue."

"Yet I must go."

"Ay, ay, there is ever a must in the mouth of a wilful man," said the friar, testily. "And then you fall sick, and it is the fault of the leech."

"That it can never be in my case," said the carver, gratefully, "for never had man a kinder or more skilful. But I will tell you why I ask. Hugh's encounter has put into my mind the thought that we might go to Dartmouth by ship."

"The saints forbid!" said the friar, rapidly crossing himself. "You must be mad to think of it, Master Bassett."

"Nay, but why?"

"The dangers, the discomforts!—shoals, rocks, pirates!"

"Dangers there are in all journeys. The discomforts will no doubt be great, but put on the other side the fatigue you warn me against."

"You should not go at all," said Friar Luke. "Remain here where you can be cared for. Hugh shall be a serving-boy, and take the habit when he is old enough."

"Wilt thou, Hugh?" demanded his father.

A vehement shake of the head was his answer.

"Nay, holy friar," said Bassett, with a smile; "I am bending the twig so far that the strain is great, but your proposal, I fear, would snap it altogether. But about our voyage. I am greatly inclined to Hugh's new friend. When does he sail?"

"In a week," said the boy, with some reluctance. He had not liked the voyage from Flanders, and this promised to be worse. Still he felt it incumbent upon him to show no fear.

"That would do well. I tell thee what, Hugh, thou shalt ask the master to come and see me here if he has a mind for another kind of cargo."

With his usual hopefulness, the idea had taken hold of the wood-carver so strongly that he turned aside all remonstrances, though the prior himself came up to beg him not to be so foolhardy. But it was true, as Bassett maintained, that each kind of travelling had its dangers, and, if the sea offered the most, he felt a sick man's longing to be spared trouble, and a feverish desire for the salt breezes. Matthew, too, thought it philosophical to be above listening to the tales of sea-perils which the brethren related, it need hardly be said, at second-hand; but it must be owned that he showed no desire to extend his own travels so far as Exeter. Hugh went down the next day and talked to the master, who at first shook his head.

"Two landsmen on board? Where could we stow ye? And if we met with rough weather we should have you crying upon all the saints in the calendar. A sick man, too! How could he put up with our rough fare?"

"My father does not get frighted," said Hugh, indignantly, though pleased to be counted a landsman.

"Thou art a sturdy little varlet," said the master, looking at him approvingly. "If my Moll had been a boy, I should have been content had he likened thee. But I would not have her other than she is, and thou wast good to her the other day. I'll come and see thy father, and if he is a good, honest man, and none of your dandy long-toed fops, he and thou shalt have a passage to Dartmouth."

The next day was Sunday, and, to the scandal of the grey friars, Matthew insisted upon taking Hugh to St. Bartholomew in Smithfield, the noble Norman church of the Augustinian friars. There was a good deal of jealousy between the orders, and each was ready enough to listen to or to repeat tales which told to the discredit of the others; so that, as Matthew said, black, white, and grey, each held their colour to be the only one in which a friar might travel to heaven. Mass being over at St. Bartholomew's they went to great St. Paul's.

This was in that day a splendid Gothic church, twice as big as the present building, and with a dazzling high altar. But, in spite of its magnificence, and perhaps partly on account of its size, it was a notorious haunt of cut-purses and brawlers, and all manner of crimes were committed in the church; so that a few years before the king had given the Chapter leave to surround it with walls and gates, treating it indeed as a town, and keeping out suspicious characters.

By this means matters had mended a little, but there was still a great deal of unseemly conduct which caused scandal to the more devout. Hugh came back to the monastery bursting with all he had to tell, and he was beyond measure delighted when his father said he would himself go out the next day.

Before the sun had mounted high enough for Friar Luke to allow this the master of the *Queen Maud* arrived, and Stephen saw a sturdy, sunburnt man, with an open countenance, blue-eyed, light-haired, wearing a garment of coarse cloth which reached to his knees, who looked as uneasy at finding himself in a monastery as a freshly-trapped pony from his own wilds of Dartmoor might have looked in a walled town. His discomfort made him surly, so that he gave the carver no encouragement for the voyage.

"Hard living and a perilous life, my master."

"That does not affright me."

"Because you know it not," said the other, impatiently. "Here you sit in a drone's hive and hear the winds blow outside, and have no fear. With a plank for your wall you would tell a different tale."

"I have tried the plank," said Bassett, with a smile. "Though, as you say, Master Shipman, we know not other's lives till we try them, and maybe you, if you lived here, would think more kindly of what you call a drone's hive."

"The Church and the Pope swallow up all a poor man's savings," said the sailor, less gruffly. "'Tis nothing but fresh taxes, and these Lombard usurers are every whit as bad as the Jews. I would the king could make as clean a sweep of them. To make money without working for it is a sin and a shame."

"The king does what he can."

"Ay, does he," said the other, heartily. "He is the poor man's friend."

"Truly."

The sailor looked at him. "Why, then," he said, "if thou lovest King Edward—"

"No question of that."

"E'en come along with us. I am but taking down some bales of cloth and of silk, and as thou mindest not a rough life, and I have a fancy for thy boy, we may perchance rub along together."

So it was settled, and, in spite of the friar's forebodings, Stephen Bassett thought of his venture with an excellent heart. Hugh was naturally fearless, and, though the sea was a great object of dread in those times, he believed his father knew best, and began to look forward also. But first he would have Bassett come forth for his promised walk, and without Matthew.

"He has been very good to thee," said the carver reproachfully.

"Ay, but he has always something to say against everything. This might be better, or that couldn't be worse. I believe he would find fault with King Edward himself."

"Poor Matthew! He has the critical spirit," said Stephen, smiling.

"Is that what makes him so thin?" demanded Hugh, innocently.

"Ay. It often works that way, and is bad for the owner. Nevertheless, it has its advantages. Look at that bowl. If I listened to the good brothers I should deem it perfect; but when Matthew says, 'Hum—I know not—is there not something lacking?' I begin to search for a way of bettering it, and presently find that he was right. So his fault-finding does me a better service than all their praise. Keep that in mind, Hugh. Now we will forth. I will buy some cloth and take it to one of the tailors' guild, that you may have a cloak for rough weather like mine."

This was a delightful errand, and when it was ended Stephen had not the heart to refuse Hugh when he begged that he would try to go towards St. Paul's and see the noble church. The boy was very happy in acting as showman, pointing out the beautiful spire while they were yet at some distance. He had begged to bring Agrippa, promising to keep him covered by a piece of cloth, and the monkey was sufficiently alarmed by the strange noises and cries in the street to keep quiet. Hugh found it a rare opportunity to ask questions which Matthew had been either unable or unwilling to answer.

"Look, father, look quickly! There is a woman with bread in her panniers! What is she doing?"

"I have heard of her," said Stephen, stopping. "Friar Luke told me that, instead of folk being forced to fetch the daily bread from the bakers, there was now a woman who had got leave to take it round from house to house. She has the thirteenth loaf for her pains. Truly there's no knowing to what a pitch of luxury we may come! Are we nearly at our journey's end, Hugh? My legs have fallen out of the way of walking, and are true sluggards."

'IS HE HURT?'   p. 72.

He was in truth standing somewhat exhausted in the road under one of the black-timbered houses in Ludgate Hill, when a small cavalcade of knights and squires, some in armour, some in the scarlet cloaks of the Hospitallers, came sharply round the corner, so sharply, indeed, that in the narrow road one of the squires' horses struck Stephen and sent him staggering against the wall.

The party reined up at once. Hugh had uttered a cry and sprung to his father's side, dropping the monkey as he stretched out his arms. Half a dozen men-at-arms crowded round; one of the red-cloaked knights leaped from his horse, but they all drew back before one who seemed the principal knight, a man of great stature, with brown hair and thick beard, and gravely searching blue eyes.

"Is he hurt?" he demanded. "That is your squire's rough riding, Sir John de Lacy."

"My liege, 'twas but a touch," urged an older knight. "I saw it all. He can scarce be hurt." Stephen, indeed, had well-nigh recovered himself, though dizzy with the shock, and scarcely knowing what had happened or why he was surrounded by horsemen. Hugh, seeing him revived, stared at the group with all his might, while the monkey, frightened to death at the horses, had run up a projection of the house and perched himself upon a carved wooden balcony, from which he scolded and chattered.

"It is nothing, I am not hurt," faltered Stephen; and then the colour rushed back to his white face, and he bent his knee hastily. "My Lord the King," he stammered, "is it not?"

"Ay," said Edward, with one of his rare kindly smiles; "but it was not I who rode over thee. Art thou not hurt?"

"Nay, my liege, it is but that I have been ill. It was no more than a touch."

It had all passed quickly, but a knot of bystanders had by this time collected, kept off by the men-at-arms.

"He speaks truly, my lord," said one of the Hospitallers who had dismounted. "He has not been hurt by the horse, but—"

He paused significantly, and Edward glanced at Hugh. "Come hither, boy."

So Hugh, crimson with wonder and delight, stood by the king's horse, and answered his questions as firmly as he could. His father was a wood-carver. They were going to Exeter to seek work—by ship, as he took care to state; and meanwhile, because father had been so ill, they were lodging at the Franciscan monastery in Newgate Street.

"And is that thy beast?" asked the king, whose quick eye had caught sight of the monkey between the carved work of the balcony. "How wilt thou catch him? Let us see."

Hugh promptly stood under the balcony, opened his arms, and uttered a call, to which Agrippa responded, though fearfully, by swinging down by tail and hands and dropping into his master's arms.

"Well climbed indeed," said Edward; and seeing that Stephen was in some degree recovered, he bade one of the men-at-arms lend him his horse and go with him to the convent. "And here is a gold piece for thee, boy—for remembrance," he added, tossing him the coin as he moved off.

"And a silver one for the monkey," said a young knight, with a merry laugh, stooping to offer the mark to Agrippa, who cleverly clutched it, and then trotting after the king.

All had passed so quickly that Hugh scarcely knew where he was or what had happened. He stood staring at the gold noble in his hand, while the bystanders closed up curiously, and one rough fellow, who looked as if he had been drinking, made as though he would have snatched it from his hand. A fat monk, with a red good-natured face, hit the fellow a sound buffet; the crowd laughed, and the man-at-arms made haste to get Bassett on his horse, and to hurry his charges away, the king being always roused to anger by any brawling in the streets.

"Keep close to me," he said to Hugh; "and give thy money to thy father. Now, where are we bound? The Grey Friars? I warrant me they brew good ale there, and supper-time is nigh enough to make a tankard right welcome."

"And that was the king," said Hugh, drawing a deep breath.

"Ay, the king. What thinkest thou of him?"

"I would I could fight for him," burst out the boy.

"Why, so thou shalt!" said Hob Trueman, with a laugh. "Eat good beef, and drink good ale, and grow up a lusty yeoman. The king's a good master, I have nought to say against him—saving that he is somewhat over strict," he added, with qualifying remembrance. "We should be near by this time—"

That night, before lying down in the wooden crib which served for bed, Stephen Bassett called his boy.

"Hugh, thou hast not forgotten thy promise," he said anxiously.

"No, father;" in a low voice.

"Fight for the king thou must, or be ready to fight. That is the law for all Englishmen. Does not that content thee?"

Silence. Then—"I should like to be near him, to be one of the men-at-arms."

Bassett sighed.

"I cannot yield to thee, Hugh."

"No, father."

"And I have no breath for talking to-night. We will speak of it again."

Chapter Five.

The Voyage, and what came of it.

Stephen Bassett was not the better for that day's work, though the accident was too slight to have harmed a man in fair health, and it made a sound reason for Friar Luke to urge upon him that he should give up his wild project of going west in the *Queen Maud*. But the carver was, if possible, only the more bent upon the scheme. He wanted to get Hugh out of London, where was more stir of arms and rumour of wars than in the shires, and have him safely bound apprentice where there should be no withdrawing.

"He will not fail me, poor little lad," he said; "but were I to be taken from him here his task would be ten times harder. Besides, I see no opening for him except what the good brothers offer, which he would hate worst of all."

So he kept the tales of his aches and weakness to himself as much as he could, though it cost him not a little to avoid Friar Luke's reproachful eye when he came in from the garden with his herbs; and, armed with a letter from the prior—written in Latin on a strip of vellum—to the head of the Franciscans in Exeter, and accompanied to the water's edge by several of the brethren, and a hospitable store of provisions with which they insisted on supplying them, the little party and their gear got safely on board the vessel, and would go down the river by the next tide. Little Moll and her mother were there, which made it seem more friendly to poor Hugh, who looked about him with dismay, and had had all possible mischances put before him by the friars, who thought Bassett's action nothing less than flying in the face of Providence.

Still, when the farewells had all been spoken, the cumbersome anchor dragged out of the mud, and the great square sail with its sprawling centre device rigged up, they went merrily down the river. It was getting towards the middle of October, and the great buildings of London, the Abbey of Westminster, the Church of the Templars, the Gothic spire of St. Paul's, the Tower, and various beautiful conventual buildings, stood, mostly surrounded by fine trees, in all the glory of autumnal gold and red. The lesser buildings—the very hovels—were picturesque, the river ran clear and strong, the vessels flaunted bright sails, colour was everywhere, and the soft blue mists but made a fair background for the scene.

Stephen Bassett stood watching, with a feeling that it was for the last time, when Andrew the ship-master joined him.

"A fair prospect," said the carver.

"Ay, though I love my red Devon hills better. But, tell me, master, is it true, as thy boy relates, that you met King Edward yesterday and spoke with him?"

"I said not much, I had no breath left in my body," said Stephen, smiling; "but it is true that the king spoke to us, chiefly to Hugh, and was very gracious."

"To think of that!" said the sailor, staring. He walked away, but after this it was evident that his respect for his passengers was mightily increased, and he seldom came near Stephen without putting some question as to how the king looked and spoke, while Hugh had the same to answer from them all—more, indeed, since he never tired of the subject, and his pride in it was immense. His father had sewn his gold piece into the lining of his vest; Hugh never intended to spend it, it was for "remembrance," as he was never tired of telling his father; and Stephen used laughingly to inquire whether Hugh had begun to persuade himself that he had been the hero of some courageous adventure, for reward of which the king had bestowed the token upon him? The boy used to redden at this, for there was a certain truth in the jest, and finding himself listened to with such interest by the sailors was like to turn his head.

Fortunately, as usual, there was a depreciating element. The youngest on board was a round-shouldered somewhat misshapen lad of seventeen, ill-favoured in temper as well as face, unpopular among his mates, except for one gift, that of storytelling. He could relate or invent tales with amazing ease, and on days when there was an idle calm the men, who at other times knocked him about roughly, would listen spell-bound for hours. This was his moment of glory.

But on this voyage his power seemed gone. The real explanation was very simple: the wind had shifted so as to follow them favourably, they had got safely round the dangerous Goodwins, and swept down the Channel past Dover, its castle and old British church standing out sharply above the white cliffs, while the setting sun shone like fire on the great sail of the vessel. They cast anchor in the first convenient creek; this required care and labour with the oars to avoid shoals, and the men were too sleepy afterwards to listen to stories. So it went on; the breeze blew freshly from the east, Stephen, crouched under what shelter the stern could afford, shivered, but Andrew the master rubbed his hands, and there was no slackening sail or delay.

This was really the reason why the sailors would not listen to the boy Jakes, but he chose to lay it to Hugh's charge.

"Young fool," he muttered, "always boasting, and telling about the king, I wonder they hearken!"

Such spite as he could work he was not slow to show. Many rough practical jokes he played, which Stephen counselled his boy to receive good-humouredly. But Hugh was set up with his Ludgate Hill adventure and the notice it had brought him, so that it made him mad to be jeered at for feeling sea-sick, or tripped up over ropes, or brought to the ground when he imagined himself to be sitting on something solid. Jakes was afraid of Agrippa, never having seen a monkey before, and fully sharing the idea that here was something uncanny, which was quite able to revenge itself if any harm was attempted. Jakes, therefore, let him alone, and even preferred to play his malicious jokes upon Hugh when the monkey had climbed the ropes and was out of reach and sight.

The voyage had on the whole been a success, and the *Queen Maud* was at length coasting along under the white cliffs of Dorsetshire, with the red ones of Devon lying rich and soft against a blue grey sky before them, and the sea leaping and whitening under the easterly wind.

"Strange that it should blow so long at this season," said the master, standing by Bassett and looking forwards.

"If it goes on, we may get in to-morrow night?"

"Ay, if it doesn't freshen into a gale, which the saints forbid! I mind not a gale in my teeth, but rocks before and the wind driving behind is what I mislike. Methinks, master," he added, abruptly, "it will be well for you to get to your journey's end."

"I have a longer before me," said Stephen, with a smile.

"Ay, to Exeter," answered Andrew, misunderstanding, "and I have been thinking I would put you ashore at Teignmouth, and save you a piece of your journey. I might try Exmouth, but—there are ill tales of Exmouth, as I told you there were of Dartmouth," he added, with a laugh; "at Dartmouth they know me, but at Exmouth—there might by chance be a mistake."

Stephen thanked him heartily, saying, and truly, that the shortening of the road would be a great gain. They put in that night at a small harbour formed for the convenience of coasting vessels, but though their start was made with the first glimmer of dawn, Jakes, who generally had to be aroused by a rope's end or a kick, had been on shore, and came back carrying a bag and grinning from ear to ear, so that Hugh was forced to ask him what he had got.

"Apples," he said, still grinning; "rare fine apples. Bide a bit, and shalt have one."

Hugh, who loved apples as well as any boy with a wholesome appetite should do, kept an eye on Jakes and his promise without suspecting that there might be anything unfriendly in this sudden change of disposition. The wind had freshened, of that there could be no doubt, and the sailors were busy with the lumbering sail, when Jakes beckoned Hugh forward to the bow, where was the bag.

"Put in thy hand and pull'm out, quick!" he said, running back to his work; and, thinking no harm, Hugh thrust in boldly, to have his fingers instantly seized in a nip which made him feel as if by the next moment they would be all left behind in the bag.

He cried out lustily, and dragged out his hand, to which a fine blue-black lobster was hanging, a creature at least as strange to Hugh as the monkey was to Jakes. The more he shook the tighter the lobster pinched, and when one of the sailors looked round the sail he could do nothing but split his sides with laughing. Hugh, crimson with pain and fright, was dancing about, vainly trying to disengage his hand. Jakes, the next to appear, broke into uproarious merriment.

"Ha, ha, ha!" he yelled, "told him there were apples in the bag, and he went for to steal 'em! Serve him right, serve him right! How like you your apples, my master?"

The buffeting of the wind in the sail and the rising noise of the sea had kept much of this from Stephen, but he at last became conscious that something unusual was going on, and made his way to the bows.

"Father!" cried poor Hugh, flying to him.

"Why, my little lad!" said Bassett, unable himself to avoid a smile, "what coil have you got into?"

"What is it?" demanded the boy, in a shamefaced whisper, as his father proceeded quietly to loosen the great claws.

"A lobster. Didst never see his like? He will be a dainty morsel for supper, and will change his blue coat for a scarlet. There," he added, as he finished his task, "I counsel Agrippa not to let his curiosity jeopardise his tail. But how did he fasten on you?"

"It was that wicked Jakes!" cried Hugh, with flashing eyes.

"Were a stealing my apples," Jakes retorted, defiantly. "Told him there was apples in the bag, and he put in his hand and the lobster caught un." And clapping his unshapely hands on his knees, he roared with laughter once more, until he bent himself double. Hugh flew at him like a tiger, but the other sailor pulled him off.

"Never heed the great lozel," he said. "It was but an apple."

"He told me—he told me to put in my hand and take one out," panted Hugh, struggling with his captor. "He's a false liar!"

"Softly, Hugh, softly," said his father gravely.

Jakes was for telling his story again with fresh detail, when the master's voice was heard calling angrily. Stephen got Hugh back into shelter, and Agrippa, frightened by the creaking of the mast and the straining of ropes, clambered down to take refuge in his master's arms. Hugh's face was like a thunder-cloud. He burst out presently—

"To call me a thief!"

Stephen was silent.

"If Dickon had left me alone, I would have made him own it was a false lie. I would I were a man!"

"Why?"

"I should be strong and could fight," the boy said, surprised at the question.

"I often think of that time," returned Bassett thoughtfully. "I may not be here to see it, and I would fain know—" He paused.

"What?" asked Hugh.

"Who thou wilt fight?"

"Who? Mine enemies," said Hugh, lifting his head.

"If you know them."

"I shall know them, because they will try to do me a mischief. Jakes— he is an enemy," fiercely.

"Thou hast worse than Jakes, my poor little lad," Stephen said, tenderly, "and nearer at hand. Thine own passions will truly do thee a mischief, except thou keep them under. There's fighting ground for thee. And, see here, I have long meant to say something to thee about King Edward, only I have an ill-trick of putting off. Thou thinkest the only way of serving him is by hard blows. He himself would tell thee that there be better ways. Serve the State faithfully as a peaceful citizen, keep the laws, and work for the glory of God and the honour of England. He would tell thee more. That his hardest work of government has been the task of governing himself. That is what has made him a great king. It seems small to thee just now, but one day, my Hugh, my words may come back."

A fit of coughing stopped him. Hugh's ill-temper had had a little cooling time, but it had not by any means left him. It was not the pain, perhaps it was not even so much the being called a thief, for no one on board was like to listen much to Jakes, and as for his father he had not even cared to allude to the absurd accusation. What Hugh really so much hated was the being laughed at. He had heard the men roaring with merriment after Dickon joined them, even his father had laughed; it would be for ever a sort of standing joke. What turned his thoughts more than anything was the weather. Anyone could see how much the wind had strengthened since they put out to sea. The colours, which had been clear and distinct, now had become blurred; a wet mist, not yet rain, but near it, was driving up from the southeast; the waves had grown larger and rushed past them in wild hurly-burly; the air was full of noisy tumult; the clumsy vessel groaned and laboured on her way, and Stephen and Hugh could not find shelter enough to protect them from the clouds of spray which swept across the vessel.

Andrew, the master, was too closely occupied with his work to come near them; he shouted directions to the man who was steering, but kept by the sail, and Bassett knew enough of the sea to suspect that they were in a position of some peril. For himself he thought it mattered little. He knew that he was even more ill than he outwardly appeared, and the wetting under which he was shivering was likely to quicken matters. But for Hugh? He could resign himself, it was a far harder matter to resign this young life, so full of vigorous promise— to give up with him all the hopes in which he had indulged of fame to come to his name, though not in his life. He had dreamt of late much of this; had pictured Hugh leaping to eminence, leaving his mark as a stone-carver in some beautiful cathedral, where age after age his work should stand, and when men asked who had done this great thing, the answer would be—Hugh Bassett. Was it all to end in an unknown grave under the grey waters which leaped so wildly round their prey?

Every half-hour the storm seemed to increase in fury. The shores on either side were now blotted out, and the steering was a matter of great difficulty. Andrew took it himself for a time, but his quick eye and steady courage were needed for the look-out, and he went forward again until he gave orders to strike sail. Then he once more came back and stood near Bassett and Hugh, looking as undaunted as ever. But when he spoke they could scarce hear his voice for the turmoil of the sea.

"Rough weather, goodman!"

"Ay! Will the boat hold?"

Andrew, who had stooped down to catch the carver's words, straightened himself with a laugh.

"Ay, ay, the boat will hold. No fear of her failing. But where she will carry us I would I could say so certainly. Thou wouldst fain be back in the drones' hive hearkening to book and bell, eh?"

"I am right glad to be remembered in the good brothers' prayers," said Stephen, quietly.

"Well, it may be as you say. Those I have known—I would not have given a base pollard for the pardon-mongers' prayers; but there are false loons in every craft."

They were silent again, for their voices were pretty well stormed down, and the sea broke so fiercely over the vessel that two or three of the men had to be constantly baling it out. Still she held her way gallantly. The shipmen of that day were not without an imperfect form of compass, in which the needle was laid upon a couple of straws in a vessel of water, but these contrivances were apt to get out of gear at the very time when they were most needed, such as a storm like that now raging round the *Queen Maud*, and hardy sailors trusted rather to their own skill and courage or their knowledge of the coast. Nothing was, therefore, so dangerous as fog or mist.

To Hugh, however, what seemed most terrible was the wild driving storm and the rush of the waves against the boat, which shivered under each stroke as if she had received a mortal blow. Agrippa, wet and miserable, cowered in his master's arms, and turned up a piteous little wrinkled face full of inquiry. Hugh crept closer to his father, and at last put his question—

"Shall we be drowned?"

Stephen turned and caught his hands in his.

"Nay, my little lad, I know not, I know not! I should not have brought thee!"

The boy looked in his face gallantly.

"I am not frightened," he said, "only I wish poor Agrippa were safe."

They were silent again after this. Andrew was evidently uneasy; he shouted orders to the sailors, and strained his eyes through the baffling mist as if he feared what might be in advance of him. His hope, and it was a feeble one, consisted in the chance that he might strike the estuary of the Teign, avoiding the bar, and, as the tide would be full, getting into the shelter of the river. He was one of the most skilful of the sailors of the west, knowing all the currents and dangers thoroughly; but navigation was then in its infancy, and vessels were clumsy, lumbering things, suited but to calm weather, when they would coast along from creek to creek. The bolder craft chiefly belonged to pirates. Still, England was beginning to awake to her sea powers, and Henry the Third had taken the title of Ruler of the Seas in honour of a victory gained over the Spaniards. Andrew himself had been down as far as Spain, and was held to be over-daring; moreover, he wanted to hasten his voyage and get back to his wife and to Moll, otherwise he would hardly have put out that morning in the teeth of a possible gale.

And now, although nothing was to be seen except perhaps what seemed like a thickening of the mist, Stephen knew from the master's face that the danger was worse. He was so numb and cold himself as to feel indifferent to his own fate—besides, as he reflected, at the most it was but shortening his life by a month or two—but his love for Hugh went up in a yearning cry that he might be saved. He touched him, and made the boy put his ear close to his mouth.

"See here, Hugh," he said, with labouring breath, "if you are spared out of this coil thou must make thy way to Exeter. The Franciscans will take thee in at first, but thou must seek out James Alwyn. I mind me that was the name of thy mother's cousin. Get him to apprentice thee where thou canst learn thy trade. Thou hast it in thee—do not forget."

"No, father," said poor little Hugh, glancing fearfully round.

It was but a minute after that, or so it seemed, that they heard a cry from one of the sailors. The wall of mist had suddenly become solid; it loomed before them in unmistakable cliffs, so near that the man who was steering dropped the rudder and fell upon his knees. With a cry of rage Andrew leaped back from the bows, seized the rudder, and using all his strength forced her head somewhat round. It was a strange sight, this struggle of the man with the elements. The man standing undaunted in the midst of a hurly-burly which threatened quick death, facing his danger without flinching, resolute, bent upon snatching every advantage which skill could give him. That the vessel was drifting against the wall of red rock before them was plain; Stephen, clutching Hugh in his arms, wondered that the master should hope to avert it. Suddenly he saw Andrew's face change. He set his teeth, and slackening the rudder drove straight for the cliffs.

There was a breathless pause; the next minute the vessel struck a small sandy beach, driven up it and wedged there by the uplifting force of the waves. The master's keen eye had noted the one comparative chance of safety, and had tried for it. Almost as the ship touched the sailors sprang forward and leaped into the sea. Only Andrew, Bassett, Hugh and Agrippa remained on board.

Chapter Six.

A Weary Journey.

The first sensation had been one of deliverance. The second was more like despair.

The waves breaking against rocks and shore looked more terrible than out in the open sea, and this sudden rush for safety on the part of the men had something about it so cowardly that it produced in Stephen a wretched sense of desolation. He supposed that in another moment Andrew would have followed his fellow sailors, and they would be left alone. Andrew had in fact rushed to the bows as the men leaped over, and Stephen, bitter in spirit at such a cruel desertion, strained his boy in his arms so that, if he could do no more, he might at least hide death from him.

He almost started when he heard a voice. The master was standing over him with a face full of rage.

"The cowardly loons!" he cried; "I would the waves had choked them! No Devon man would have played such a trick. I knew they were helpless oafs, but to save their skins like that! If they had stopped it would have been easy enough, but now we must think how to get thee on shore." Stephen sprang up.

"Think not on me. My life is nothing. Save Hugh, and I ask no more."

Andrew stared at him and began to laugh.

"Prithee, dost thou suppose I should leave thee here to drown? Why one of thy precious drones' hive would scarce be so unmanly, though, in truth, I can say nought against them after those base knaves of mine. But now, see here, if I fasten a rope round the mast—which will hold yet awhile—and go ashore with the other end, canst thou find thy way?"

"The boy first."

"Ay, the boy first, and the monkey with him, if the beast has the sense to hold on. Thou wilt want both hands for thyself, Hugh."

"I will tie him to me," cried the boy, hopefully. His hopes had risen with Andrew's cheerfulness, and as for Bassett, with the revulsion of feeling, a new and extraordinary strength seemed to have come to him; he helped the master to fasten the rope securely, and stood, unheeding the buffet of wind and waves, watching the sailor when he had cast himself into the sea, and was fighting his way towards the shore. Once or twice he was sucked back by the retreating water and nigh overwhelmed, and the time seemed endless before they made out that he had gained a footing, and was with the other men on the beach. His shout only faintly touched their ears.

"Now, Hugh," said Bassett firmly.

They had bound poor Agrippa as closely to him as they could, while round his own neck the carver had disposed a bag with money and such small specimens of his workmanship as were portable. His tools he was reluctantly obliged to leave behind him; his breathing could bear no further weight.

"Thou wilt be sorely scratched by Agrippa," he said. He was so hopeful he could smile. But the monkey was so cowed that he only clung closely, turning his head piteously from side to side, and realising that something terrible was about to happen. Hugh bore himself manfully.

One or two of the sailors who had escaped, finding themselves safe, were ready to help Andrew with the rope, and though the boy was half choked and sorely beaten by the waves, he held on, reaching the shore after a tremendous tussle, by the end of which he was so spent that he fancied he must drop, when he felt himself clutched by Andrew and drawn through the remaining waves. He lay for a time exhausted on the beach; but life was young and strong in him, and he staggered to his feet, tried to comfort and warm the poor monkey, and to watch for his father's coming.

THE SHIPWRECK.   p. 95.

Andrew had scarcely thought that Bassett would have the strength to bear the passage through the surf. It relieved him greatly to find that the carver was slowly nearing the shore. Now and then he disappeared under the crest of a great wave, but he always reappeared, holding on with a tenacity which was little less than miraculous. Andrew, though even his strength was pretty well spent, again cast himself into the sea to help him in his last struggle, and the carver by his aid managed to reach the shore, but in so terrible a plight that Hugh cried out and flung himself by his side.

And now a very dreadful thing happened, for, as Stephen lay there like a log and Hugh knelt calling on him to look up, the waves, which had but just had their prey snatched from them, as if they meant to show that in another case they had had their way, brought up something large and dark and motionless, and flung it at their very feet; and while Hugh, scarcely recognising what it was, yet shrank from it as from some fearful thing, two of the men ran hastily down and seized and dragged it beyond the water's reach. Hugh caught the face then, and gave a cry of horror; it was the boy Jakes—dead.

He must have swooned after this, for when he came to himself again he was lying higher up, at the mouth of a small natural cave formed in the sandstone rock. His father sat by him, and in the cave a fire of brushwood had been lit, close to which crouched Agrippa, munching black rye bread soaked in sea water, and jabbering with satisfaction.

"Father," said the boy, sitting up and rubbing his eyes, "are we safe?"

"Saved by a miracle, my little lad."

"But Jakes—his face—what was it!"

"He was drowned," said Bassett, gravely; "he never got to land with the others. Eat some of this bread; I had it in my pocket."

"Is anyone else drowned?" asked Hugh, shuddering.

"No, thank Heaven! And the master has gone off to see if perchance there might be some hut or cottage near where we can get lodging for the night and means of reaching Exeter."

"Father, you must be spent. Think no more of me. Sit by the fire, and take off your clothes to dry."

Hugh was almost himself again, although evidently deeply shocked at the death of Jakes, and with the burden on him of remorse for unkind thoughts which is hard to bear. But fire and food comforted them all in some measure, and Andrew came back before long to tell them that he had been lucky enough to reach a serf's hut not far away, where they could at least find shelter, with hope of a horse.

"You have done everything for us, and have lost more than any," said Bassett, gratefully.

"Nay, I know not what I have lost yet," returned the sailor. "The bales of silk and woollen are spoiled; no hope for them. But maybe, if the gale goes down, I may have my boat again. I can put up with the rest."

When they had rested awhile they made their way up through a sort of gully piercing the red cliffs. This same redstone amazed Hugh, for the pools of rain were crimson to look at, and he had never seen anything like it before. But glad enough he was to turn his back on the wild sea.

"I hate it! I would I might never see it again."

"Thou wouldst be a poor crusader," panted Stephen, whose breath was sorely tried by the ascent.

They stumbled on through tussocks of grass until they reached the top, where trees grew thickly, though somewhat one-sided and windblown with south-west gales. Andrew was not with them, but he had directed them fully, and they soon came upon a rough hovel, built of a mixture of mud and straw called cob, and coarsely thatched. A wild-looking herd and a wilder-looking woman stared at them from the doorway; but though uncouth they were not unkindly, and had got a fire of logs burning, together with bread and bacon and a large tankard of cider on the table.

As usual, the monkey caused the greatest astonishment, and Hugh dared not loosen his hold of him because of a sheep-dog, who growled angrily at the strange party. The other sailors were already there, eating and drinking and drying their clothes, and presently Andrew came in. He was very short and surly with the men, though, as he told Stephen afterwards, unable to cast them off altogether, as he would willingly have done, because, if there were a chance of saving the boat, he would need their help in getting her off and in sailing her. All depended upon the abatement of the gale. If the wind went down with the tide there was a chance of floating her in calmer weather and of repairing damages. She was strongly built, and, so far, showed no signs of breaking up.

To Hugh's eyes his father seemed scarcely worse or more feeble than he had often been before. He was very pale it is true, his breathing was laboured, and he had a short, sharp cough, which scarcely ceased; but he was keen to push on, and would not rest until he had urged the herd to go that evening to the sheep-farm where he worked, and where he thought a horse might be bought. They were, as Stephen ascertained, not more than fifteen or sixteen miles from Exeter, the spot where they were wrecked being a little north of the mouth of the Teign; and this he was feverishly anxious to declare they could ride in a day. A strong horse could easily carry two; it was madness for him to think of remaining where he was for rest, since if he became worse there was no means of procuring a leech.

"E'en go thy way," said Andrew, half angrily, half sadly, for he had done enough for his passengers to feel a sincere liking for them.

The hut, as usual, consisted of but one smoky room, in which they all bestowed themselves for the night. Andrew saw that Stephen had the best of the miserable accommodation; but little rest came to him owing to the constant torment of his cough, and he was up as soon as the sailor and out in the air, though not strong enough to go down to the cove. But what a change was there since the former night! The wind had shifted to the south-west, and blew as softly as if it had never known violence. The sun, though not yet showing much face through misty grey clouds, filled the air with delightful promise. All the land colouring was rich and varied, for the trees, though shaken by the past storm, were in their fullest and most gorgeous autumnal colouring, and the deep red of the soil, the vivid green of the grass, and the brown of the bracken made a splendid harmony of tint.

The sailors followed the master to the cove; the herd went off to his work, promising that the horse should come when the morning was a little advanced, after the nine o'clock dinner; the wife made much of Hugh; and Stephen, looking and feeling wretchedly ill, tried to wear off his restlessness by wandering towards the edge of the cliff, but his strength giving out he was forced to crawl back and sit quiet. The horse arrived, and proved a strong, serviceable beast.

Stephen could scarce touch the coarse food, being too feverish. Andrew came up quite hopeful, and laden with the carver's tools and other possessions, which, though somewhat marred by the salt water, he was thankful to see again. The woman of the house dried the clothes; all the gear was securely strapped on the horse, and then came the farewells. The master would not consent to receive a penny for the cost of the voyage.

"Nay," he said, "we feasted on the grey brothers' good cheer, and, by my troth, I shall never have the heart to call it a drones' hive again. One of these days Moll and I will go and have speech with Friar Luke, and let him know what befell. Nay, I tell you, I can be obstinate too, though with no hope of evening thy powers in that matter. Wonderful it is that so little mischief has been done with all that turmoil; if the poor fool Jakes had but stayed on board he would have saved his skin."

"Have a mass said for his soul," said Stephen, pressing a little money into his hand. "Nay, thou must not refuse, it is conscience money."

"Well, it shall go to the grey brothers," said Andrew, who seemed to limit his new-born tolerance to the one monastery. "Hearken, Hugh, if thy father is spent, get him to stop for a night on the road. Some day I shall come to see thee at Exeter."

The kind-hearted sailor stood watching the pair when they had started, Stephen riding, Hugh stepping manfully through the bracken, and both turning back and waving their hands until they were lost in the thicket of underwood through which they had to pass before reaching the road.

Road, indeed, it could scarce be called, for at this season the best were in some places nigh impassable, and Devonshire mud when it is left to follow its own will cannot easily be beaten. In sortie parts the road was little more than a channel worn by constant running of water, and leaving banks on either side; and, owing to the rain of the day before, the water flowed down these banks in little runnels, and rushed cheerfully along the course at the foot. Hugh, however, found it amusing enough to splash through these streams, or to leap from bank to bank, and clamber along through ivy and long grasses and briars and nut-bushes; such a thicket of greenery as he had never seen before. When he was tired he would scramble up behind his father, the stout grey making light of his double burden; and he was untroubled by Stephen's anxiety lest these narrow lanes should offer opportunity for thieves and outlaws.

They met no such dangerous folk. A ploughman passed and looked curiously at them, and a priest carrying a staff, and on his way to a sick parishioner, stopped and inquired whither they were bound. Bassett's evident illness made the good man uneasy, and he would have had him rest at his house until better able to go on; indeed, pressed it on him. The carver shook his head.

"I thank you heartily, sir priest, but I must push on, having, as you may judge, but little time before me. If, of your courtesy, you will point out the shortest and safest road, you will be doing us a kindness."

The old man, who had a very pleasant and earnest face, assured him that, so far as he could tell, the country for some miles round was tolerably free from rogues, though he could not answer for the neighbourhood of Exeter. He himself went a little way with them, and directed them the shortest path along the rocks, where the sea stretched on one side, softly grey, and only a little stirred with remembrance of yesterday's gale, and pointed out Exmouth, which he said had an ill character for pirates, and then showed them the Exe stretching away, and told them how they should leave it on their right and take the inland road, and so left them with his blessing.

It was all that Stephen could do to hide his increasing weakness from Hugh. There were times when he felt that he must give it all up, drop from the horse, and let himself die by the road-side. Only a will strong for his boy's sake could have given him strength to sit upright. When they paused at a little hostelry for some food he did not dare get off his horse, fearing that he might lack the resolution to mount again. His suffering became so acute that he could not hide it from Hugh, and though the boy dreaded nothing worse than one of those sharp fits of illness which his father had weathered before, he did his best to induce him to seek a night's lodging on the road. But Stephen refused almost irritably.

Nor could he bear to follow where Hugh's remorse would have led him—into talk of Jakes. It seemed as if he would put aside all that was harsh and painful, and he was either silent or—as the boy afterwards remembered—let fall words which showed that his thoughts were with the wife he had lost, or dwelling upon some of the talks he had had with Friar Luke. Once or twice Hugh was sorely perplexed by what he said, fancying that he could not have heard rightly; but Stephen seemed unable or unwilling to repeat the sentence, and murmured something else. Once they fell in with a gay party going to a neighbouring castle; there was a minstrel, and two or three glee maidens were of the company. When they overtook Stephen and Hugh they were making a great noise and merriment, and the boy wondered why, on seeing them, all their jests died away and they looked almost frightened. They made haste, too, to part company, saying they had no time to spare; and Hugh saw them looking back and pointing as at some strange sight.

He was beginning to be alarmed himself, though not knowing why, perhaps chiefly because his father seemed to heed him so little, no longer asking if he were not tired, or noticing Agrippa's merry pranks, but riding bent upon the horse's neck, and seeming only to keep his seat with difficulty. Hugh called gladly to him when he saw before him a town which he guessed to be Exeter, lying on a hill above the river, with the fair cathedral standing in a very beautiful position about half-way up, and Stephen so far roused himself as to clasp his hands and to murmur, "God be thanked!" but with that fell back into silence.

It was well that the road was plain enough to need no consultation; and poor little Hugh, wearied out, for he had ridden but little of late, thinking it oppressed his father, struggled manfully on, hoping to get in before sunset. It was well, too, that the last mile or two was of a tolerable flatness, and the road wider and less heavy, though always bad; for Stephen grew more and more bowed, and Hugh became so fearful lest he should fall that he had to steady him as he walked by his side.

Thankful he felt when he came upon a few scattered hovels while the sun was yet some quarter of an hour from setting, at which time the town gates would be shut, and presently he saw the river running swiftly, swelled by the autumn rains, and spanning it a brave new bridge of stone, with houses and a chapel upon it.

"Father, father, here is Exeter!" cried Hugh, with anxious longing for some reassuring word.

But he got no answer, and not daring to pause lest the gates might be shut, he joined the throng of citizens who were pressing in for the same good reason, and passed through the gate before setting himself to ask questions. The first person he addressed gave him a shove and told him to get out of his way; but the second, who by his dress and bearing might have been some kind of trader, stopped at once, and having satisfied his own curiosity as to who they were and where they came from, showed himself of a most friendly nature.

"We are in the Western or High Street," he said; "we have come through the West Gate, and the Franciscans have their house between this and the North Gate. But thou art a little varlet to have so much on thy hands, and thy father looks in a sore plight. A monkey, too! How far have you come?"

"Some sixteen miles, noble sir."

"Nay, I am no noble; only plain Elyas Gervase. Sixteen miles, and a dy— a sick man who can scarce keep on his horse! What doth he work at?"

"He is a wood-carver, sir."

"Why, that is somewhat my own craft, since I am a stone-cutter. Have you friends in this fair town?"

"Father has a letter to the prior, and I am to seek out a cousin of my mother's, Master James Alwyn," said poor Hugh wearily.

"The child himself is almost spent," muttered the good citizen to himself. "Prothasy would make them welcome, and we are surely bidden to entertain strangers. Thou and thy father shall come home with me," he added aloud, laying his hand kindly on Hugh's shoulder. "My house is nigher than the monastery, and I will speak to a learned leech as we pass. Both of ye need a woman's care."

If the boy was a little bewildered at this change of plan he could not oppose it, nor had he any desire to do so. There was something in Master Gervase's honest face which instinctively inspired confidence. He was a man of about forty-five, somewhat light as to complexion and hair, his beard was forked, his eyebrows were straight, marking a kindly temper, and his eye was clear and open. He wore an under tunic of blue cloth, with buttons closely set from the wrist to the elbow of the tight sleeve, tight pantaloons, and low boots with long pointed toes. His hair hung a little below his ears, and was covered by a cap. He walked up the steep Western Street by the side of the horse, passing his strong arm round poor Stephen's bowed form so as in some measure to support him, and he paused presently before a door, and sent in a boy to say that Master Gervase prayed Master Miles to come without delay. A few minutes after this they stopped again before a timbered house projecting far into the narrow street. Without a moment's delay Gervase had lifted Stephen from the horse, and rather carried than led him in.

"Prothasy!" he called, the moment he was in the passage.

"I am coming!" answered a voice, and, following the sound, a young woman ran in, small, dark, bright-eyed, and scarcely more than a girl in appearance. "How late thou art, Elyas! And whom have we here?" starting back.

"A sick man for thee to nurse. Nay, thou shalt hear more later, when we have got him to bed. Wat! Where's Wat? Wat," as a lad hastily appeared, "go out to the door and take the horse, and see that he has good food and litter. Send the boy that is there in here."

It was evident that Prothasy Gervase was a capable woman. She asked no questions, made no difficulties, but ran to see that all was right, and Stephen, too much exhausted to be aware of what was happening, was got into his crib-like bed in a little room overlooking the street, and Mistress Gervase had brought up some hot spiced wine and bidden Hugh take a drink of it before the doctor came. Then Elyas took the boy down to the common room, and asked him a number of questions. He was one of the burgesses who, by a recent law, was responsible for the good conduct of twelve—some say ten—citizens, and would have to furnish an account of the strangers, so that besides the call of natural curiosity, to which he was not insensible, it was necessary that he should know something of their history. He listened attentively to the story of the shipwreck.

"And what brought thy father here?" he asked at last.

"He thought," faltered Hugh, for his spirits had sunk low, never having seen his father in such sore plight before, "that our cousin, Master Alwyn, might help him to get work in the great church of St. Peter's."

"James Alwyn is dead," said Gervase, gravely. Hugh's face quivered. He seemed more lonely than ever.

"He died a year ago, come Martinmas. What was thy mother's name?"

"Alice Alwyn."

"I mind me there was one of that name lived out by Clyst. And—but I warrant me thou wilt say, ay—is thy father a good craftsman?"

"There is no better work," said Hugh, proudly. "He will show it you, gentle sir, and you will see."

"Ay," said Gervase, hesitatingly, "and thou wilt follow his craft?"

"I would carve in stone," muttered Hugh, turning away that his questioner might not see the tears which sprang into his eyes. He was tired, and his heart seemed strangely heavy.

"Sayest thou so!" eagerly. "Thou art right, there is nought like it. We must see what can be done for thee, perchance—" he checked himself.

"I must talk with Prothasy," he added, under his breath.

He was very good to the boy, leaving him to make a good meal while he went out to meet the doctor, a gaunt, melancholy man, dressed in bluish grey lined with thin silk, who spoke with bent head and joined finger-tips.

"By virtue of the drugs I administered," he began, "my patient hath revived a little, but Is in evil case."

"How long will he live, sir leech?" demanded Elyas bluntly.

"Scarce more than a few days. I am going home to prepare a cordial, and I shall cast his horoscope to-night, when I doubt not to find evil influences in the ascendent."

"You may take that for granted without seeking to find out whether it is so," said the other, with a short laugh. "However, let him want no care. Will you be back before curfew?"

The doctor promised and kept his word. By eight o'clock all lights were out; Hugh was stretched on a rough pallet in his father's room with Agrippa, at whom Mistress Prothasy looked askance, by his side, and all was silent, indoors and out, save for the quick laboured breathing of the sick man.

Chapter Seven.

In the Warden's Household.

It was doubtless a satisfaction to the leech's astrological mind to ascertain that, beyond a question, malignant conjunctions were threatening Stephen Bassett. But without this profound knowledge it was evident to the watchers that Master Gervase had brought home a dying man, who would not long be spared. He rallied a little, it is true, and though at times light-headed, and always taking young Mistress Prothasy to be his lost Alice, could understand and be grateful for the kindness shown him, and speak feebly to Hugh about his work. The prior's letter had been taken to the Franciscan monastery, but no sign was given by that house of the kindly hospitality shown in London.

"I knew it," said Elyas, with some triumph to his wife. "When the boy told me whither they were bound, I could not bear they should have no more comfort than they would get from that fat prior. Now, the poor man shall want nothing."

"Truly, no," said Prothasy, quite as heartily. "But it were best that our little Joan remained away a little longer with thy mother."

"I suppose so," answered her husband, with a sigh. "The house seems strangely silent without Joan."

"We must have sent her away had she been here," she said decidedly.

He went to the door and came back.

"Prothasy," he said, with something like appeal in his voice, "that is a comely little lad."

"Ay, Elyas."

"What will become of him when his father is dead?"

"Thou hadst best seek out some of his kin."

It was not the answer he wished for, yet, as always, it carried sense with it; he hesitated before he spoke again.

"If he would be a stone-cutter?"

"Thou hast two apprentices already."

"Ay, but a fatherless child—"

"Elyas, thou wilt never learn prudence. All would come upon thee."

"The guild would help in case of need."

"So thou sayest, but never wouldst thou apply."

He made no answer, only seemed to be reflecting as he left the room. She walked quickly up and down, once or twice dropping her long dress and stumbling in it.

"Was ever anyone so good as he, or so provoking!" she exclaimed, half crying. "A fine dowry will come to Joan, when her father spends his all upon strangers! And yet he makes me cry shame upon myself for close-fistedness, and wonder at the sweetness with which he bears my sourness. If he will, he shall have the boy as prentice, I'll e'en put up with the monkey; but, do what I will, it is certain I shall season any kindness with sharp words, and Elyas will feel that all the while I am grudging. I would I had a better heart, or he a worse!"

Elyas, meanwhile, all unknowing of these stormy signs of relenting, went slowly up to the little bare room where the carver lay, while Hugh, looking out of the small unglazed window, was telling him as much as he could see to be going on in the street. Stephen, however, was paying little attention, and when Gervase came in his eyes brightened at once.

"Leave Agrippa here," he said to Hugh, "and do thou run out and look at the Cathedral, and bring me back word what it is like."

His interview with his host was long, the more so as he could speak but slowly, and at times had to stop altogether from exhaustion. Then it was necessary that Elyas should see the carving, which took him altogether by surprise.

"Truly," he said, "this will make our good bishop's mouth water! He is ever seeking for beautiful work for St. Peter's, and thou mightest have made thy fortune with misereres and stalls. Perchance—" he said, looking hesitatingly at the carver. Stephen shook his head.

"Never again," he said. "But Hugh, young as he is, has it in him. If— if he could be thy apprentice?"

Elyas almost started at having his thought so quickly presented to him from the other side, but he did not answer at once, and Stephen went on, his words broken by painful breathing—

"There is a little money put by for him—in yonder bag—I meant it for this purpose—the horse may be sold—if I thought he could be with thee I should—die happy."

Gervase was not the man to resist such an appeal. He stooped down and clasped the sick man's wasted hand in his.

"The boy shall remain with me," he said. "Rest content. I am warden of my guild. He shall learn his craft honestly and truly, shall be brought up in the holy Faith, and shall be to me as a son. There is my hand."

With one look of unutterable thankfulness the carver closed his eyes, and murmured something, which Elyas, bending over him, recognised as the thanksgiving of the *Nunc Dimittis*. He said no more, but lay peacefully content until he roused himself to ask that a priest might be sent for; and when Hugh came in Elyas left him in charge, while he went to seek the parish priest, "and no monk," as he muttered.

Hugh was full of the glories of the Cathedral, to which he had made his way. It had remained unfinished longer than most of the others in the kingdom, but the last bishop, Quivil, and the present, Bitton, had pushed on the work with most earnest zeal, and Hugh described the rising roof and the beautiful clustered pillars of soft grey Purbeck marble with an enthusiasm which brought a smile of content upon the face of the dying man.

"Would I could work there!" said the boy, with a sigh.

"One day," whispered his father, "Master Gervase will take thee as apprentice; thou wilt serve faithfully, my Hugh?"

The boy pressed against him, and laid his cheek on the pillow.

"Ay, to make thy name famous."

"No, no," gasped Stephen, eagerly. "That dream is past—not mine nor thine—not for thyself but for the glory of God. Say that."

"For the glory of God," Hugh repeated, gravely. "Father?"

"Ay."

"Where wilt thou live?"

There was a silence. Then the carver turned his eyes on the boy.

"I am going on—a journey—a long journey." Hugh shrank away a little. He began to understand and to tremble; and he dared not ask more questions. The priest came and he was sent from the room, and wandered miserably into a sort of yard with sheds at the back of the house, where the stone-cutting was going on, and journeymen and two apprentices were at work.

One of these latter—the younger—was the boy called Wat, whom Hugh had already seen. He was a large-limbed, untidy-looking, moon-faced lad, the butt of many jibes and jests from the others, careless in his work, and yet so good-natured that his master had not the heart to rate him as he deserved. The other apprentice, Roger Brewer, was sixteen, and had been for six years with Gervase, who was very proud of his talents, and foretold great things for his future. He was a grave sallow youth, noticing everything and saying little, and with a perseverance which absolutely never failed. The journeymen, of whom there were three, were stone-workers who had been Gervase's apprentices; their seven or eight years ended, they now worked by the day, and hoped in time to become masters. They wore the dress and hood of their guild, and one, William Franklyn, had the principal direction of the apprentices. Much of the stonework of the cathedral was being executed under Gervase's orders.

When Hugh appeared in the yard, Agrippa produced an immediate sensation, Wat and the men crowding round him, Roger alone going on with his work of carving the crockets of a delicate pinnacle. The boy's eyes glistened as he glanced about at the fragments which were scattered here and there, while the others, on their part, were curiously examining the monkey.

"Saw you ever the like!" cried Wat, planting himself before him, all agape, with legs outspread and hands on his knees. "Why, he hath a face like a man!"

"Ay, Wat, now we know thy kin," said one of the men, winking to the others, who answered by a loud laugh.

"Where got ye the beast?" asked William, laying his hand on Hugh's shoulder.

"At Stourbridge fair," answered the boy. He had to give an account of their adventures after this, and they stared at him the more to hear of London and the shipwreck.

"And so thy father is sick to death in there?" said another man, pointing over his shoulder with his thumb. The tears rushed into Hugh's eyes, and Franklyn interposed.

"His craft is wood-carving, they say. Hast thou learnt aught of the trick of it?"

"Nay, I shall be a stone-carver," faltered the boy. "I am to be prenticed here."

"With Master Gervase?"

"Ay."

William Franklyn looked black. He had a nephew of his own whom he had long tried to persuade the master to take into his house. That hope was now altogether at an end. He turned away angrily and went back to his work.

"What wilt thou do with thy monkey?" cried Wat, hopping round in high delight.

"No foreigners may work in the yard. That were against the guild laws," said one of the men. "Down with all Easterlings!"

They were a jesting, light-hearted set, who laughed loudly, lived rudely, had plenty of holidays, yet did excellent work. At another time the boy would have had his answer ready, but now was sick at heart, and wanting nothing so much as a woman's comforting, and the men thought him sullen. He got back to his father as quickly as he could, leaving many remarks behind him.

"An ungracious little varlet!" said one.

"Tut, man, he could scarce keep back his tears," said another who saw further.

"What makes the master take another prentice? I thought Mistress Prothasy would never abide more than two. And there was thy nephew, William, if a third must be."

"The master will do what pleases him," said Franklyn stiffly.

"Or what pleases Mistress Prothasy, and most likely this is her fancy. She would have another Wat in the house."

This was followed by a loud laugh, for Wat's awkwardnesses were well-known to bring him into sore disfavour with the mistress of the house.

The day went by, and the night came on again. Elyas proposed sitting up himself, but Stephen refused, saying that he wanted no one but Hugh.

"And I think I shall sleep well," he added, with a feeble smile.

Afterwards, Gervase thought he meant more than his words conveyed.

Before Hugh lay down his father made him put back the shutter from the little window, and look out upon the night. All was quiet, lights were extinguished, every now and then the watchmen came up and down the street, but no other noises were abroad; the opposite houses rose up so closely that from the balconies it looked as if it were possible to touch hands, and over head, though it was late autumn, the moon shone in a serene sky, sending her silver rays into the narrow street and intensifying all the shadows. Stephen listened, while Hugh told him just what he could see.

The boy closed the shutter and would have lain down, but Stephen called him feebly to his side.

"Remember," he whispered, with difficulty. "For the glory of God."

"Ay, father."

"And the—enemies. Fight the right enemies."

"Ay, father."

Something the carver murmured, it might have been a blessing, but Hugh caught only the word, "Alice."

"Shall I get thee aught, father?"

"Nay. Lie down—I will call if I need aught."

It was his last self-denial for his child. The boy was soon asleep, but through the long hours, Stephen lay, fighting for breath, until the struggle ended in unconsciousness, and that, too, passed into death. When Elyas came in the early morning, and saw what had happened, he lifted Hugh in his strong arms and carried him into the room where the other boys slept. Wat was snoring peacefully with open mouth, but Roger was awake, and the master hastily whispered how it was to him.

"Keep the boy here. Tell him his father must not be disturbed," he said.

It was Prothasy who, after all, broke the tidings. She shrank from it at first, saying that Elyas was tenderer in words and less strange to Hugh, but her husband looked so grieved that, as usual, she repented, and did his bidding. And she was really kind, leading him in herself to look upon the peaceful face of the dead, and soothing his burst of tears with great patience and gentleness.

The days that followed were strange and miserable to poor Hugh. He had never been without his father, who had been father and mother both to him, and had made him so close a companion that in many ways he was much older than his years. And, in spite of all kindness, the sense of solitude and loneliness that swept over him when the funeral—which the guild of which Elyas was warden attended—was over, and he was back in the house, with a new life before him, to be lived among those who were, in good truth, strangers, was something which all his life long he could not forget.

The good master had him rightly enrolled as his apprentice, and then judged it well to leave him alone for a day or two, telling him he might go where he liked until his work began. No place seemed so comforting to Hugh as the Cathedral. He would go and watch the workers, and feed his keen sense of beauty with gazing on the fair upspringing lines and the noble sheaves of pillars, and wonder whether the day would come when work of his should find a place there, and his father's dream be fulfilled.

Chapter Eight.

Difficulties.

It was about a week after this that Master Gervase in working dress went out into his yard. Dinner was over at an early hour, and the two meals of the day were long and plentiful as to cheer; so long and so plentiful, indeed, that there is a record in the preceding reign of thirty thousand dishes being served at one feast, and the sumptuary laws which regulated excesses in dress and food do not seem to have been uncalled for.

In Master Gervase's household there was no excess, but abundance in every kind, and hearty partaking of beef and cider, Mistress Prothasy being famous for her housekeeping and capable ways, so that Elyas went into his yard with all the contentment of a well-fed man.

Men and prentices were hard at work in their different ways. Franklyn and Roger had the finest cutting, and Elyas paused before Roger's crocket to examine his progress.

"It is excellent," he said, heartily, so that the lad's sallow face flushed; "the cutting deep and clean—naught can be much better in sooth than the workmanship. Thy design is not so good."

"No," said Roger, quickly.

"No. It wants freedom, boldness, it smacks too much of the yard and too little of the artist. There is thy stumbling-block, Roger. I can give thee the means of execution, but I cannot put this into thee. See!"

He seized a piece of burnt stick which lay by, and on a rough plank hastily sketched a crocket similar in form to that on which Roger was working. But what a difference! What strength in the up-curved lines! What possibilities seemed to blossom out of the rapid outline! As Roger watched a look of bitter mortification gathered in his face; the ease and vigour of the drawing were, as he recognised, quite beyond his grasp. When the master moved on he drew the board close to him, yet so that it was concealed from other eyes, and tried with all his skill to bring his carving into better harmony with its spirit.

Gervase glanced at all the work in the yard, giving a word to each, and special praise to a canopy which Franklyn and another man were engaged upon, and which was an order from a neighbouring abbey.

To a fourth worker, Peter Sim, he pointed out that his moulding was thin and wanted richness.

"Ay," muttered his neighbour, "he is so thin himself he can see no beauty save in leanness."

"That will scarce be thy failing, Hal," said Gervase, good-humouredly. "Now, Wat, what tool is that thou art using?"

"It is broken, but it cuts well enough, sir," said Wat, regarding his half chisel with affection.

"Cuts well enough," repeated the master, angrily, throwing the tool on one side; "and what thinkest thou, prithee, the guild would say if I suffered such a tool to be used in my yard? And how came it broken?"

"There never was such a one for breaking his tools," grumbled Franklyn, who had picked up the chisel and was examining it; "it is my belief he uses them to dig the ground with."

"Nay," said Wat, scratching his head, "but the stone is hard."

"Thou shalt spend thy next holiday in finding out whether it be hard or not," said Elyas, angrily, "an thou be not more careful. How now, Hugh, what work have they set thee to?"

The good man's heart melted as he looked at the boy, who seemed a sad little figure among the others. He had got into a far corner, and Agrippa peered down from a rafter in the shed.

"Why art thou in this dark corner by thyself?" demanded Elyas.

"They like not Agrippa, sir," said Hugh, listlessly.

Elyas looked vexed. His wife was also sorely set against the monkey, and he would gladly have had it away, yet he could not find it in his heart to deprive the boy of his only friend. He stood awhile watching Hugh work, and presently went across to Franklyn.

"See that no harm comes to the monkey," he said in a tone which all might hear; then, in a much lower voice, "that is hard work thou hast set him to do."

"He must learn his craft," said Franklyn, gruffly.

"But he is a little urchin."

"The more need he should begin at the beginning."

"His father told me he had a wonderful talent for his age."

"Fathers ever think their children wonders. Is it your pleasure, Master Gervase, that I treat him differently from any other prentice?"

"Nay, nay," said Elyas, hastily, and, knowing that the idea of favouritism would make Hugh very unpopular, he pushed the matter no further.

The time that followed was full of bitterness to Hugh. Franklyn, though not a bad-hearted man, was sore and disappointed to have his nephew, as he thought, supplanted, and, since he could not visit it upon the master himself, he visited it upon Hugh. The other men sided with Franklyn, and Hugh made no efforts to gain their good-will; pride grows quickly, and he had been a good deal set-up on board the ship, although Jakes's death had shocked him into a temporary shame. His self-importance was sorely wounded by finding himself treated as absolutely of no consequence, he, who had spoken, as he reflected with swelling heart, with King Edward himself. Mistress Prothasy was sincerely desirous to pleasure her husband, but she loved not boys, classing them all as untidy and unmannerly. It had been by her wish that Elyas had hitherto abstained from taking more than two apprentices, and, as she was proud of her influence over him, she had made it a matter of boasting when talking to gossips whose husbands were more wilful. She hated having to put up with what she now took to be their pitying smiles, and, without meaning to be unjust, her feelings towards Hugh were not friendly. It provoked her, moreover, to have the monkey, which she both feared and disliked, in the house, and she was constantly urging Elyas to send it away.

But what Hugh felt sharply was Franklyn's treatment of him as of one who must be taught the very beginning of his craft. He had learned much from his father, and had been made to use his tools when he was scarce six years old, so that in point of fact he was advanced already beyond Wat, who had gone through three years' apprenticeship. But of all this, and in spite of the master's hints, Franklyn was doggedly unheeding. He allowed the boy nothing but the roughest and simplest work. He explained with provoking carefulness each morning how this was to be carried out, and if, as frequently happened, the boy was inattentive, he rated him sharply. The discipline might have been good, but injustice is never wholesome, and feeling himself to be unfairly treated, Hugh set up his back more and more, took no pains to please, and moped in solitary corners.

Elyas saw that things were moving wrongly, and was vexed, but he never willingly interfered with Franklyn's rule, and having an easy-going genial nature was disposed to believe that with time and patience things would right themselves. He had ever a kindly word for Hugh, though not realising how the boy clung to him as to a link with that past which already seemed so far away and so happy.

The weeks passed and November was well advanced. There was no lack of holidays and feastings, which Hugh in his present mood found almost more irksome than work. Agrippa was his chief companion, and yet his greatest care, as the monkey, if he took it with him, was ever likely to call a crowd together, and perhaps get pelted, until one day Elyas, coming upon him in one of these frays, advised him to have a basket and carry him thus, by which means he was able to take him to the cathedral itself.

Wat was not unfriendly. He was awkward and ungainly, and ever falling into disgrace himself, but this afflicted him scarcely at all. He had a huge appetite, and stores of apples, nuts, and cakes, which he was ready enough to share, and could not understand that anything more was wanted for happiness. Hugh, caring little for these joys, despised Wat's advances, and would not be beguiled into friendship. He was very miserable, poor boy, and inclined to wish that he had stayed with the Franciscans in London, as Friar Luke counselled, or to long—oh, how earnestly!—that his father had suffered him to accept Sir Thomas de Trafford's offer and be brought up in the good knight's household. As for learning his craft, that, he said bitterly to himself, was hopeless; he was more like to forget what his father had taught, and to sink into such coarse work as Wat's. In fact he made up his mind to the worst, and would scarce have been contented with easier measure.

Towards the end of November a new personage came into the family, small in size but of immense importance, Mistress Joan Gervase, aged five, who had been for some time staying with her grandmother, and had remained so long, owing to an attack of measles, or some such childish complaint. Great preparations were made for her home coming; Mistress Prothasy had the rooms furbished, and made all manner of spice-cakes, and Elyas rode off one day in high spirits, to sleep at his mothers and to bring back his little daughter on the morrow.

It was a bad day for Hugh. He was sick of his work, and, instead of setting himself to do it as well as he could, all went the other way; careless chippings brought down Franklyn's wrath upon him; he would take no pains, idled and played with Agrippa, and was altogether unsatisfactory. Franklyn had good reason for anger, though rather too ready to jump at it, and he was rating the boy loudly when Mistress Prothasy came into the yard to deliver some message with which she was charged from her husband.

It was an expressed wish of his that she should never interfere with the conduct of the prentices at their work. Indoors she might say what she liked, and nothing displeased him more than a sign of disrespect on their part, but in the yard it was understood that she was silent. Nevertheless, on this occasion she asked Franklyn what Hugh had done, and hearing that Agrippa was in the matter burst out with her own grievances.

"The hateful little beast, I would he were strangled! I am frighted out of my life to think of what he may do to Joan! But I will not bear it. Hark ye, Hugh, thou wilt have to dispose of him. I have threatened it before, and now I mean it, and I shall tell thy master that it makes thee idle over thy work. He or I go out of the house!"

She swept away, leaving Hugh in a whirlwind of grief, bewilderment, and anger. Part with Agrippa, his one friend? Never! And yet—he knew from experience, and the men often spoke of it—Master Gervase never gainsaid his wife. He dashed down his tools, caught Agrippa in his arms, and faced Franklyn in a fury.

"You have done nothing but spite me, and I hate you!" he cried. "You may kill me if you like, but I will never part with my monkey!"

In his heart of hearts Franklyn was sorry that things had gone so far, but such rebellion could not be overlooked, and he fetched Hugh a sound buffet which made him tingle all over, told him the master should hear of it, and that he should have no supper but bread and water. Hugh sullenly picked up his chisel and went on with his work, paying no heed to Wat's uncouth attempts at comfort. Work was to be put away some hours earlier than usual, and a feast provided for supper in honour of Mistress Joan's return; but Hugh would go no farther than the balcony which ran outside the prentices' room, supported by wooden posts, and here he crouched in a corner, hugging Agrippa, weeping hot tears of rage and turning over in his mind possible means of escape.

He had heard tales of prentices running away from harsh masters, although he had an idea that dreadful penalties were due for such an offence; but he thought he might manage to avoid being re-taken, and cared not what risks he ran. Where should he go? If he could get to

Dartmouth someone might keep him till Andrew the shipman came again and took him back to London, and the boundless hope of childhood made the wild plan seem possible as soon as it came into his mind. He had the king's gold noble sewn into his clothes, and though he never intended to spend it, the feeling that it was about him gave him a sensation of riches. He had received his first month's pay, as apprentice; this amounted, it is true, to no more than threepence, but Elyas had given him two groats from his father's store, and he hoped that people would be willing to pay something when he had got far enough to let the monkey display his tricks without fear of detection.

All these plans he made hastily, for the more he thought over the matter the more determined he was to run away at once. He must slip out of the gates before sunset, and while Elyas was absent; there would be so much excitement in the house with Joan's return that he would not be missed until it was too late to follow him. Wat had gone off to see some men in the pillory; Hugh hastily rolled his father's things in a bundle, slipped Agrippa into his basket, and was out of the house without meeting a soul.

He could not help pausing at Broad Gate to look through it once more at the Cathedral, but something in the beautiful building, some memories of his father's hopes, brought such a choking lump into his throat that he turned hastily away, hurrying down the Western Street and out at the West Gate, and flattering himself that he had passed unnoticed by the keeper of the gate.

From one cause or another he had not gone that way since the evening they entered a month ago. Here was the new stone bridge; there in its midst stood the fair chapel where lay the good citizen who had given the bridge to the town, a little light burning ever before the altar. How well Hugh remembered touching his father's arm to show it to him, and how he got no sign in return, and was frightened. And then but a minute or two later Master Gervase had come to their help like a good Samaritan, and he no longer felt so lonely.

It was an inconvenient recollection, because he could not help recalling with a rush how thankful his father had seemed when he came to himself, and knew in whose house they were. Also with what earnestness he had prayed Master Gervase to take Hugh, telling him that he was a good boy and would be a credit to him.

"But father never knew!" cried Hugh, stifling uneasy thoughts; "he never thought I should be set to fool's work, and flouted at, and Agrippa taken away."

He pushed on with the thought. He fancied that he remembered a house some five or six miles away, where the woman had been kind, and would have had them come in and rest. This was the place where he meant to spend the night.

But travelling in November was harder work than a month earlier. The road soon became a quagmire, lain began to fall, darkness set in, and there was no moon. He trudged on as bravely as he could, but he began to be very much frightened with the loneliness and the darkness, and the uneasy sense that, unlike the time when he passed before, he was not going the way in which he could expect the overshadowing Care in which his father had rested so confidently. Then more than once side roads branched off; he was not sure that he was keeping to that which was right, and little as he seemed to have to steal, there was the king's gold noble which would be excellent booty for any cut-purse. The house seemed so long in coming that he began to think he must have passed it in the dark, and when at last he made it out, his heart sank to think that after all his efforts he had got no further; besides, there was not a light or sign of life about it, it looked so gloomy and forbidding that he was scarcely less terrified at it than at the lonely road. He ventured at last, however, to knock timidly at the door, but was answered by such a fierce growling that he clasped Agrippa the closer and fled.

Fled—but where to flee? Wet to the skin, hungry, miserable, before he had got six miles on his way, what could he do? Creeping back to the house to see if there were no outside shelter under which he might crawl, he at last found a small stack of fuel piled close to the mud walls, and by pulling this out a little formed a small hole where he made shift to lie, shivering, and in a miserable plight.

He slept, however, and forgot his misery until he awoke, cramped, aching all over, and hungrier than ever. He was too much afraid of the dog to venture to wait till the people were up and about, and set off again on his weary tramp, hoping he might reach some other hut where he could get food for himself and the monkey. Rain still fell, though not so heavily, and he could not understand why he got on so slowly, and found himself scarcely able to drag one leg after the other. Agrippa, too, also wet, cold, and hungry, shivered and chattered piteously.

At last he reached a hut where the man had gone to work, and the woman gave him black bread and cider. But she had an evil face, and took more from him than the food was worth, casting greedy looks at the remainder, and the children ran after him and pelted him and

Agrippa with stones; so that Hugh was forced to hurry on as fast as his aching limbs could carry him, and by the time he had gone up a little hill, felt as if all the breath were out of his body, and he must drop by the road-side. He knew now that he must be ill, it seemed to him, indeed, that he was dying, and it was horrible to picture himself lying unheeded among the piles of dead leaves, the dank and rotting vegetation, the deep red mud—no one would know, and his only friend, poor Agrippa, would die of cold and hunger by his side.

It was no wonder that his thoughts went back with longing to Master Gervase's house in Exeter, where food and shelter were never lacking.

After this he still struggled on, but in a dazed, mechanical sort of way, until he was quite sure that he had been walking all day, and that night must be near at hand. And with this conviction, and all the horror of coming darkness sweeping over him, he felt he could go no farther, and flung himself down upon the wet bank, under a thick growth of nut-bushes.

There Master Gervase found him.

When Elyas reached home close on sunset the day before, there was so much welcoming and hugging of Joan, so many messages to give, so many things to be spoken about, that he did not at first miss Hugh, especially as Wat was also absent. By-and-by when Wat returned, open-mouthed with sights at the pillory, Elyas asked for the little boy, and Prothasy poured out her grievances. The monkey made him idle, and she had said it should not stay in the house, and then he had flown into a rage with William, and had been told he should have nought but bread and water.

"And that is better than he deserves," she ended. "Look you, husband, I am resolved. That evil beast shall not remain here with Joan. Thou knowest that my nay is ever nay."

Elyas looked very grave, but made no answer. Hugh was idle, and no rebellion against Franklyn could be permitted, yet his kind heart ached for the fatherless little fellow who had taken his fancy from the first. He would not interfere with the punishment, but he resolved that when supper was over, he would go upstairs and see whether he could not mend matters. And he was a little distraught throughout the long supper, whereat Joan reigned like a veritable queen, and, it must be owned, tyrannised in some degree over her subjects. She rather vexed her mother by demanding the new boy. Father had talked to her of him, and had told her of a wonderful little beast with a face like an old man's, and hands to hold things by; she would love to see him— where was he, why didn't he come to supper?

"Think not of him, Joan," said her mother quickly at last. "He is no playfellow for thee. He would bite and terrify thee."

This caused an interval of pondering, and Prothasy fondly hoped of impression, but presently Mistress Joan lifted her little golden head.

"I want him," she said. "I would kiss him." Prothasy looked reproachfully at her husband, who was smiling.

The supper, as has been said, was long, and before it was finished Joan, tired out with excitement, was leaning against her father's arm, asleep. He lifted her tenderly and carried her to their room, where she slept, and where she was soon lying in her little crib, looking fairer than ever. Husband and wife stood gazing at her with overfull hearts, and Elyas, ever large in sympathies, let his thoughts go out to the wood-carver who had cared so much for his boy, and wished he could have taken Hugh with him that day, or that he could talk him into readier obedience to Franklyn. He was very desirous to temper justice with mercy when he left Joan and went to seek Hugh.

It surprised him exceedingly to get no answer to his call. He lifted the light and looked round the room in vain, nor was Agrippa to be seen overhead among the rafters. It was possible that Hugh had slipped out and stayed thus late, but he had never done it before, and it was seven o'clock, dark and raining. Elyas began to feel very uneasy. He sought his wife, called Franklyn, who had not left the house, and questioned the other apprentices. Roger never paid any attention to Hugh, treating him as a little boy, whom it would be waste of time to notice; Wat reported that he had invited him to go out with him, but got no answer.

"He had never seen a man in the pillory, either, and here were three," added Wat cheerfully.

Quick compunction seized Prothasy, though rather for her husband's sake than Hugh's; she said little, but ran hastily about the house, and even out into the wet yard, where, however, Franklyn had been before her, and then she stood in the doorway, looking up and down the street. Her husband's voice behind startled her.

"He hath run away," he said gravely.

"Thinkest thou so?" she said turning quickly. "Elyas, it was not much that I said, and it was not he but the monkey which provoked me."

"Nay, I am not blaming thee, I blame myself. He is but a little lad to be left friendless in the world, and I might have been more tender with him, and kept him more by mine own side. Then this would not have happened."

"Where will he go?"

"That I must find out at the gates, which I will do presently, though it is too late to pass out to-night. Most likely he has taken the road he knew best."

He came back before long, saying it was as he thought, for the keeper of the West Gate had seen the boy go out. At sunrise Elyas said he would mount his good grey and follow. There was nothing else to be done, and he made as light of it as he could to Prothasy, saying the dreariness of the night might give a useful lesson.

And so it was that early the next day, when poor Hugh had got no further than a bare two miles from the place where he had slept, although he felt as if he had been walking all day, Master Gervase came upon a little figure lying under a clump of nut-bushes, and with a pang in his heart, sprang off his horse, and gathering Hugh and Agrippa into his arms, mounted again, and rode back as quickly as he could to Exeter.

Chapter Nine.

Bishop Bitton in his Cathedral.

Hugh's illness was severe and painful, for he was racked with feverish rheumatism, and could scarcely bear to be touched or even looked at. Often he was light-headed and talked persistently of his father, imploring him not to leave him, and at other times would cry so bitterly that it was impossible to soothe him. Prothasy had been terribly shocked when her husband rode up to the door, carrying his unconscious burden, and had spared neither care nor attendance upon him, rigidly carrying out the directions of the leech, which to us would sound hopelessly fantastical, and listening patiently to his long disquisitions upon Aesculapius and Galen. But her presence seemed to disturb the boy, and she often drew back wounded. Strange to say, he endured Wat's awkward though good-hearted ministrations, but the only person to whom he clung, to please whom he would take his medicine, and who seemed to have the power of causing him to sleep, was Elyas. One possible reason was that Master Gervase had a strange quickness in finding out what troubled him. Once or twice he had soothed him by putting before him his father's carvings, and more often by placing Agrippa on the bed. The monkey had been ill himself after the exposure of that night, and it was Prothasy who—mightily it must be owned against her inclination—wrapped him in woollen, and though she could never be brought to take him on her lap, saw that he was not neglected.

'DOTH HE BITE?' p. 143.

But one day, when Hugh was really better and less feverish, though still in pain which made him fretful and peevish, he opened his eyes upon a new sight. A little girl, with golden hair and brown eyes, stood about a yard away from the crib, gazing with deep interest and her finger in her mouth, from him to Agrippa, who sat on the bed in his scarlet coat, and stared back at her. For a short time all three were silent, contemplating each other curiously. It was Joan who broke the silence, pointing to Agrippa.

"Doth he bite?"

Hitherto everyone who came near Hugh had asked how he felt or what they could do. Here was a change indeed!

"No." Then with an effort—"You may stroke him, mistress."

Upon this invitation Joan advanced, stretching out two rosy fingers. But they hesitated so long on the way that Hugh put forth his own wasted little hand, and conducted them to Agrippa's head. Joan coloured crimson but would not show fear.

When she had got over the wonder of this courageous deed, she began to smile, bringing two dimples into her cheeks, and dancing a little up and down for joy.

"Art thou the new boy? Why doesn't thou get up?"

This was too much; besides, the pain of stretching his hand had hold of him. Hugh shut his eyes and groaned. The next thing he felt was a dreadful shake of the crib, and a soft kiss planted upon his closed eye.

"Poor boy! Make haste and get well!"

She trotted away, but the next day appeared again, and her mother, arriving in haste, found to her horror Joan sitting upon the edge of the crib, with Agrippa in her arms. Prothasy would have snatched him from her, but Joan put up her small hand lest she should come too near. She was actually trembling with ecstasy.

"He doesn't bite, and he likes me. Isn't he beautiful?"

Agrippa had conquered.

After this Hugh began to improve more rapidly Joan's visits brought something into his life which had been wanting before, and he could not but be conscious of the kindness with which he had been nursed and cared for, when he might have expected very different treatment. He still watched Mistress Prothasy with anxiety, but his eyes followed Gervase with devotion which touched the good warden's heart. Nothing had been said about Hugh's flight during the worst part of his illness, but one afternoon in December, when Elyas had come in from consultation with the bishop at the Cathedral, he sat down on the boy's bed.

"We shall have thee up and about by Christmas," he said, cheerfully; "out by the New Year, and at work by Twelfth Day."

"Ay, master," said Hugh faintly.

Elyas turned and looked at him. "It were best for thee," he said, "to tell me what ailed thee that day. I have heard nothing from thee."

In a faltering voice Hugh would have murmured something scarce distinguishable, but Gervase made him put all into words. It is often hard so to describe one's wrongs; things which had seemed of infinite importance lose dignity in the process, and there is an uncomfortable conviction that our hearers are not so greatly impressed as we desired. After all, except the threat about Agrippa, it looked trifling seen from a distance, and even for Agrippa—

"Hadst thou met with so much unkindness here, that thou couldst not trust us to do what was best?" asked Gervase gravely.

"I thought—" began Hugh, and stopped.

"And how came you idle?" Elyas demanded more sternly.

"He ever gave me such foolish work! He would not hearken when I said I could do better!" burst out Hugh. "Master, only let me try, and you will see."

"Perhaps," returned Elyas. "But there are things that I value more, ay, and thy father would have valued more, than fair carving. Thou hast got thy life to shape, Hugh, rough stone to hew and carve into such a temple as the Master loves. All the best work that we can do with our tools is but a type of this. And what sort of carving was this rebellion of thine?"

He would say no more, being one of those who leave their words to sink in. But after, when he came up to see the boy, he would choose for his talk tales of men who had become great through mastery of themselves. And when he found how Hugh's thoughts ran upon King Edward, he spoke of him, and how he had tamed that strong nature of his which might have led him into tyrannical acts, so that at whatever cost to himself he followed faithfully that which was right and just. And he told the story of how once, when he had been unjust towards an attendant, he punished his own hasty temper by fining himself twenty marks.

"This it is which makes him great," added Elyas.

"And thou hast seen and spoken with him? The more need to follow him."

"Saw you ever the king, goodman?"

"Ay, truly; ten or eleven years ago he and the queen held Parliament here at Christmas. Great doings were there, and it was then the bishop got leave to fence the close with walls. I like them not myself, they shut out the fair view of the western front; but after the precentors murder the chapter sought greater security. There is talk of the king coming again next month. If he does I warrant he will bring a sore heart, remembering who was with him last time."

"And the queen was fair, goodman?"

"Fair and sweet beyond telling. All that looked at her loved her."

Hugh never got worse reproach for his conduct, but by listening to these tales of Master Gervase's with talk of men who took not their own wild wills, but a high ideal of duty for their standard, he grew to be ashamed of it, and to have a longing for the time when he might go to work again in a different spirit. And he changed in his conduct to Wat, who was ever full of awkward good-will.

It was much as Elyas had foretold. By Christmas time Hugh was up, though too feeble to enter into all the merry-making and holiday-keeping of the time; nor, indeed, could he so much as go out with the others when, at two of the morning, the moonlight shining, the rime hanging to the elms and just whitening the roof of the Cathedral, they all set forth for the parish church of St. Martin's. Wat came back blowing his blue fingers and stamping on the ground, but radiant with the promise that next year in the mumming he should be St. George himself.

"Rob the ostler says so, and he knows."

"Thou wast the hobby-horse last night," said Hugh with a laugh.

"Ay, and I am weary of the hobby-horse, of prancing up and down, and being hit with no chance of hitting back again. But, St. George! what wouldst thou give, Hugh, to be a knight all in shining armour, and to slay the Dragon?"

New Year's Eve was the great day for gifts; Joan had a number of toys and sweetmeats, and Hugh gave her a kind of cup and ball, which he had managed to carve for her, though with trembling fingers, after the recollection of one which had been shown to his father by a merchant travelling from China, or Cathay, as it was then called. It was a dainty little toy, and Gervase examined it closely, feeling that Hugh had some reason for fretting against the monotonous work to which Franklyn condemned him. But Elyas had no thought of interfering. He believed it would be wholesome discipline for the boy to have to work his way upward by force of perseverance and obedience, each step so taken would be a double gain; he had time enough before him, and should prove his powers to Franklyn by his own efforts. Meanwhile he kept him with him a good deal, and took him one day to the Cathedral to see the progress which had been made.

Hugh could not rest without going everywhere, and then was so tired that, while Gervase went off to inspect some of the masons' work, he curled himself up upon one of the misereres and fell asleep. He awoke with a start to find himself looked down upon by a kindly-faced man in an ecclesiastical dress, though this last was not of the sumptuous character at that time worn. Other ecclesiastics were moving about the building. Hugh started to his feet, but the priest, whoever he was, seemed in no way displeased at his presence.

"Thou art a pale-faced urchin," he said good-humouredly; "have thy friends left thee behind and forgotten thee?"

"Nay, reverend sir," said Hugh, "I am Master Gervase's apprentice."

"I always heard he was an easy man, and so he suffers his apprentices to sleep in working hours? But it is he for whom we were searching, and if thou wilt go forth and find him for me, thou mayest earn a silver penny."

Hugh had some little difficulty in discovering Elyas, who had climbed a scaffolding to examine the work close at hand. He hurried down when he had heard Hugh's report, saying that it was doubtless the bishop, and bidding the boy follow him.

The three bishops who succeeded each other in the see of Exeter, Quivil, Bitton, and Stapledon, have each left their mark upon the Cathedral. Quivil's share was the most important; it was he who by the insertion of large windows formed the transepts, and to whom we owe the beautiful and unbroken line of vaulting. Bitton was only fifteen years at Exeter, but he carried on the designs of his predecessor with enthusiastic loyalty, and completed the eastern end of the choir. It was this on which he constantly desired to consult Gervase.

"The work goes on well," he said cheerfully, rubbing his hands. "You have caught the true spirit. We shall never see our glorious Church finished, goodman, yet it is something to feel that we shall have left behind us something towards it. *Quam dilecta tabernacula tua, Domine virtutum!* I like the lightness of that stonework, and mine eye is never weary of following the noble lines of vaulting. Only I shall not rest until something has been designed to unite it with the pillars. There is a blank look which offends me."

"I see it, too, my lord. Is it not the very place for a richly carved *surs* (corbel)?"

"Ay, that is it, that is it! A corbel which should spring from the pillar, and follow the line of the arch. We must reflect on this, Master Gervase, and they shall be of finest cutting, and each varying from the other. But we may not think of this yet awhile, for truly there is enough on hand to call for all thy skill and industry. How fair it looks, with the winter sunshine striking on the fair stonework! *Non nobis, Domine!*"

One or two of the canons had by this time closed up, and began to speak of what had been done.

"When the western end is brought to equal the eastern," said one of them, William Pontington by name, "there will be no church in our land more fair. What will the king say?"

"The king is not in the best of humours with his clergy," said the chaunter or precentor, a little dried-up man, with a sour face. "What think you, my lord, of the archbishop's mandate?"

The good bishop looked uneasy. Winchilsey, Archbishop of Canterbury, was a turbulent and ambitious prelate, and the king, though sincerely religious, was forced to be ever on the watch against encroachments made by Pope Boniface, and supported by the archbishop, which threatened the royal supremacy. The strongest attempt of all had just been put forth in a bull from the pope, "forbidding the clergy to grant to laymen any part of the revenues of their benefices without the permission of the Holy See." Now as the kings of England had ever the right of taxing the clergy with the rest of their subjects, as the possessions of the Church were enormous, and papal taxation of the whole kingdom far exceeded the taxation by the State, so that in a few years the pope is said to have received money from England equal to nine millions of our present money, Edward promptly resisted this fresh and unheard-of claim. He did so by a simple and effectual counter-stroke. It was announced at Westminster that whatever complaint was brought to the court by the archbishops, bishops, or clergy, "no justice should be done them," and this withdrawal of State protection speedily led the clergy to offer their submission to the king, in spite of the anger of pope and archbishop.

But the dissension had placed them on the horns of a dilemma, and Bishop Bitton had no liking for speech on the subject. He muttered something in answer to the precentor's injudicious question, and turned to Hugh, who was standing a short way from the group.

"There is thy penny for thee," said the bishop, beckoning to him, "and now tell me, sir apprentice, whether thou art a good lad, and learning thy craft fairly and truly, so that in time thou mayest have thy share in this great work of ours?"

Hugh coloured crimson, and looked down, and Elyas came to his rescue.

"He hath not been with me yet three months, my lord, so please you, and half that time hath been ill; but he is the child of the wood-carver of whom I spoke, and, if he is industrious, I have good hope he will credit his father."

"And what part wilt thou choose for thy share?" asked the bishop, with a wave of his gloved hand towards roof and walls.

"The corbels, my lord," answered Hugh, boldly. Bitton looked delighted.

"So thou hast caught our words, and wilt bespeak the work thyself? Well, I shall not forget. Learn with all thy might, and, who knows, some day thy carving may help to decorate this our Church of St. Peter's?"

After this, when the bishop caught sight of Hugh, he never failed to speak to him and ask how his learning fared. And hearing from Elyas that the boy could read and write, he arranged that on Sundays he should come to the Kalendarhay, where one of the Kalendar brothers instructed him.

When Twelfth-Night was over, Hugh went back to the yard, where work was expected to go on vigorously after the feasting and mirth of that season, which was loud and boisterous. On the eve the town was full of minstrels, who carried huge bowls of wassail—ale, sugar, nutmegs, and roasted apples—to the houses of the well-to-do inhabitants, and Wat, as it may be conceived, had his full share in these doings. In the country there was a curious pagan ceremony kept up in Devonshire on this night, for at the farms the farmer and his men would carry a great pitcher of cider into the orchard, and choosing the best bearing tree, walk solemnly round it, and drink its health three times.

Master Gervase grew somewhat red and shamefaced when his wife reminded him that he had often been the pitcher-bearer on his father's farm.

"It was there I first saw thee," she said, "and my mother pointed thee out, and said thou wast as strong as Edulf."

"Who was Edulf?" asked Hugh of Wat, under his breath.

"The strongest man that ever lived. He came to Exeter in a rage, and broke the iron gate with his two hands," expounded Wat, stuffing a large piece of pasty into his mouth.

"The strongest man that ever lived was Samson," said Hugh, dogmatically.

"Samson! Nobody ever heard of him, and I tell thee Edulf was the strongest."

The quarrel might have grown, but that Franklyn growled at them to hush their unmannerly prating; and Joan announced in her clear, decided voice that Agrippa should have his special Twelfth-night spice-cake. For in spite of her mother's loud remonstrances, the monkey had been taken into Joan's heart of hearts, and, it was certain, was secure from any sentence of banishment.

Franklyn had been a good deal shocked by Hugh's flight and illness, but, as was natural, the impression passed away as the little apprentice regained his health, and Elyas saw that he was not inclined to change his treatment. For the reasons already given, the master had no thought of interfering, it was for the boy now to prove what stuff he had in him. It was a sort of ordeal through which he had to pass; an ordeal which might develop patience, resolution, and the humility of a true artist, and though Gervase told himself that he would be on the watch, ready with words of encouragement when they were needed, he held back from more. Hugh had the same rough, uninteresting work to toil upon—indeed the stone had been set aside for his return; the same careful explanations of how to handle his tools and make his strokes, which he took to be a reflection on his father's teaching; the same lack of praise. But now he brought to it a more cheerful spirit, hope was astir; he felt sure that the master was watching his efforts, and that it rested with himself and his own perseverance to make his way. It was not easy. Often he grew hot and angry; often he was tempted into careless work; but he would not give up trying, and upon the whole held on very fairly.

Then, in spite of his awkwardnesses and a dense stupidity about his work, Wat was a good-natured companion, ready to take any trouble and to carry any blame. He had been so often told by Franklyn that he would never rise to more than a mason, that he had grown to accept the verdict against which Hugh was always trying to make him rebel.

"He knows best," he would say, hammering loosely at the stone.

"What an oaf thou art, Wat! It all rests with thyself. Franklyn should never make me a mason."

"Because—there, I have chipped it!" scratching his head in dismay.

"And small wonder! Give me thy tool, which thou holdest as the goodwife holds her knife—so!"

"If I thought it were any use—" began the disconsolate Wat.

"Try and see."

"And thou thinkest I might catch the trick of it?"

"Try. There, now go on. Thou knowest as well as any how to hold the tools."

So far as impatience and calling of names went Hugh was a harder taskmaster than Franklyn, but he put more energy into his teaching, and dragged the reluctant Wat along by sheer force of will, the result being that, though he got no praise for himself, some fell to his pupil, which really pleased him as much as if it had been the other way.

Wat was the great purveyor of news; no one knew how he picked up his information, but nothing happened in the city but it somehow reached his ears before it was half an hour old. He knew of all the quarrels between the bishop and chapter and the mayor and his twenty-four councillors or aldermen, and how two of the canons fell upon two of the bailiffs and pommelled them vigorously, before even the mayor's wife had been informed of the scandal. He it was who reported the falling out between Sir Baldwin de Fulford and his wife, because she wanted an extravagantly fine chaplet of gold, the cost of which displeased him. It seemed that there were great expenses she led him into, for they had glass over from France for their windows, and forks for dinner, and many such luxuries, and each one Wat knew quite well—though how, no one ever knew. And at last, one day in January, when there had been a fall of snow which whitened all the roofs, and gave great joy to the prentice lads, Wat rushed in, powdered over with snow, so full of news that he could scarce keep from shouting it out as he ran, and so intent upon that and nothing else that he rushed up against Mistress Prothasy, and sent the dish of roasted apples she was carrying out of her hand. She gave him a sound box in his ear, and told him he should have no apples for supper. But even this threat could not compose Wat, well as he loved roasted apples.

"Truly, good wife," he said, breathlessly, as he picked them up, "thou must forgive me this time for my news."

"What news?" said Prothasy crossly. "Thou hast ever some foolish tale in thy idle head."

"This is no foolish news," cried Wat, triumphantly. "King Edward is on his way!"

"Nay!"

"Ay, mistress, it is true. He is at Bristol, and comes here in four days' time, and the mayor is almost out of his wits, and there will be a banquet at the Guildhall, and the Baron of Dartington and Lord Montacute and Sir Richard de Alwis and my Lord of Devon are making ready to ride to meet the king, and all the saddlers and armourers are rushing from one end of the city to the other, and there will be feasting and bonfires, and we prentices are to stand in the Crollditch to shout when he comes in at the East Gate, and I warrant you none will shout lustier than I!"

"Mercy on us, thou wilt deafen me with thy chatter!" said Prothasy, clapping her hands on her ears; "but there is an apple for thee, since thy head had some reason for its turning to-day. The king so near! I must go and pull out my green kirtle."

Chapter Ten.

Sword or Chisel?

Wat's enthusiasm found hearty echo in the house. Roger, indeed, ever self-absorbed and eagerly bent upon his own advancement, muttered something that such shows were fit only for fools and jackanapes, but he dared say nothing of the sort aloud, when even Master Gervase himself was like a boy in his delight over the occasion. Great consultations took place between the different guilds. These guilds had flourished in Exeter from a very early period, and were founded and preserved on strong religious lines. Chief and earliest among them were the merchant guilds. Craft guilds grew up later, not, as in other countries, opposed to the merchants, but under their authority, formed merely to promote and regulate matters belonging to their own crafts. Master and wardens met regularly in the common hall, and every full craftsman worth twenty shillings might be a brother. Generally there was a distinctive dress, or, at any rate, hood. The guilds took care that their members bore good characters, and there were heavy penalties for bad words, or what was called "misquoting." No one might work without leave of the wardens. No one might undersell a craft brother. The guilds arranged that all goods received a fair price, and that they were of the best quality. An excellent technical education was provided, and the tools that were used were closely inspected. Women might have part in the guilds, widows being allowed to carry on their business under their protection. There were also craft courts to which all complaints were brought, and it will be easily understood how much guilds had to do with the local government of a town.

It was now necessary to organise a banquet to be given to the king, and a day of feasting and rejoicing for the poor, and Gervase was very busy over the arrangements. Frost and snow still continued, but flags and gay hangings were profusely used, and nothing could have been more picturesque than the narrow streets with their beautiful black-timbered houses, snow on the steep roofs, and all manner of bright colours hanging from windows and carved balconies. The only thing there was doubt about was the sun, but after an hour or two of hesitation in the morning, it broke out in full brilliancy, giving the final touch to a gay pageant of moving colour, of which we in England now have little conception.

Rougemont Castle, of course, put on its gayest face, but the chief preparations were at the East Gate, to which the road from Bristol led direct, passing by St. Sidwell's Church. Here the king would enter, and here in Crollditch, the present Southernhay, where the Lammas fair was annually held, the apprentices intended to muster, and to see as much as they could, the greater number of the burgesses being within the gate, so as to welcome the king to the city. If it had not been for Wat, Hugh's chance of seeing would have been small, for as the king and his knights rode up, the bigger apprentices closed tumultuously nearer, shouting with all the force of their lungs, and the lesser boys were pushed back without mercy. But Wat was a faithful friend. He held fast by Hugh, and used his own strong limbs to good effect. Opposite to them was a crowd of the poorest of the city.

"Keep thy legs, gammer—good folk, press not so closely! Here they come!"

"Alack, alack, I can see nothing!"

"There is the king on a black horse!"

"Nay, that is my Lord of Albemarle."

"Ay, there's the king!"

"Where? Where?"

"He rides a white horse, with the bishop by his side."

"The saints preserve him! How he towers above them all! A proper man, indeed!"

The sight was very striking as the gallant cavalcade swept slowly into the grim shadows of the East Gate, with its walls stretching away on either side, and out into the keen sunshine beyond, where representatives from the guilds, the mayor, bailiffs, and councilmen were drawn up with every mark of pageantry. Loud shouts broke from the crowd, many cries of blessing were raised, and some appeals for "Justice, my Lord King!" were heard. All the way down the High Street the narrow way was so thronged with citizens that Edward and his train could scarcely make way, and there was time enough for Wat and Hugh to rush down a side way and get round to their master's house before the king reached it. Joan was in the balcony with her mother craning her little neck to see the show, and beckoning to Hugh, but the boy had a design in his head; rushing up to catch Agrippa, and, when he had got him, determinedly squeezing his way to the front. In this he might not have succeeded but for the good nature of my Lord of Devon's jester, who was a favourite in the town, and now in his motley suit had taken up his position before Master Gervase's house. He pathetically implored the crowd to make room for his grandfather, and the roar of laughter which followed when this turned out to be the monkey secured Agrippa's position.

Hugh's heart beat fast as he saw the men-at-arms clearing the way with no little difficulty.

"Hold thou on to my sleeve," whispered the good-humoured jester, "and we'll not budge."

He was as good as his word, and as the king passed with a smile on his grave face, for he was touched by the fervour of his welcome, Hugh and his monkey were so close that Edward's eye fell upon him. He was certain that he was recognised, for the king's smile deepened, and he said something to the bishop, who raised himself in his stirrups to get sight of the boy. Nor was this all. The monkey attracted the attention of the *suite*, and a knight suddenly reined up his horse and bent down.

"Why, thou art the little varlet that was at Stourbridge Fair! I mind me now thy father spoke of Exeter. How goes it with him? Has he a choice bit of his work that I can take back to my lady? What, dead! Nay, that is sad, but he looked scarce like to live. Thou mayest come to the bishop's palace, where we lie, and ask for my squire, John Wakefield, if thou wilt."

He nodded and rode on, and Hugh was besieged by inquiries of who he was, and what had led him to speak.

"Sir Thomas de Trafford," repeated the jester. "A fair name and an honourable. Prithee forget not a poor cousin, if there be preferment to be had. I would almost renounce my cap and bells to be dubbed a knight."

But Joan overhead was clamouring for Hugh, and Prothasy's curiosity was getting past bearing. She had never quite believed the boy's story of the gold noble, but all had seen the king's amused smile of recognition, and now she questioned Hugh sharply, while he was longing to be off with Wat, who was in the thick of the crowd which had closed up on the heels of the men-at-arms, and was following the king down the High Street, for to pleasure them he rode as far as the Carfax or conduit, the central point of the city, which stood at the junction of North and South Street, where much business was transacted, before going to the quarters prepared for him in the bishop's palace. Hugh got away at last, but he was in the rear of things, and could get no nearer than the tail of the procession, every now and then catching the gleam of armour in the distance as some corner was turned, while the people were cheering and pushing with all their might, and gathering the largesse freely distributed.

Gervase came home in high good humour, for the king had received the guild officers very cordially, and promised a hearing for the next day, the townspeople having certain matters to plead against the clergy with reference to the walls of the close—a very fruitful source of dispute.

"'Tis a pity though, goodman, that the king is lodged in the palace where the bishop will have his ear," said Franklyn.

"Pish!" answered Elyas. "Little thou knowest of Edward if thou thinkest him to be so easily turned! He will look into the affair and judge according to right. No favour beyond that need bishop nor mayor look for. But there is no doubt that the ecclesiastics are pushing their privileges as to right of way too far, and I wish there were as good a chance of getting Countess Weir removed, and restoring the navigation of the river."

"Father," said Joan solemnly, "I saw the king, and I kissed him my hand."

"Didst thou so, my popinjay? And I warrant that pleased him. He hath a Joan of his own, what thinkest thou of that?"

"Little, like me? Father, there was a beautiful shining knight that spoke to Hugh and Agrippa, and Hugh is to go to the palace to-morrow."

So Gervase had to hear this story. He looked grave over it, for he knew what were the boy's secret longings, and Stephen had told him of Sir Thomas de Trafford's offer, and how it had fallen in with them. And though Hugh was his sworn apprentice, and could not be removed, yet the king, who had a high respect and liking for Sir Thomas, might ask for his release as a personal favour which the stone-cutter could not refuse. Elyas felt, moreover, that the boy's first days of apprenticeship had not been of a kind to lead him to care overmuch for his craft. Franklyn had succeeded in making them full of discouragement, and though of late Hugh had worked steadily and well, he had been given no opportunity of getting on, and might well be out of heart. Elyas felt very doubtful as to the result of this visit, and was grieved not only because his promise to Stephen had been to do his utmost to teach him his craft, but because he really loved the boy. In those days apprentices were not treated as "hands," they were actual members of the family. Roger was too self-absorbed to have won his master's affection, and Wat, though he had excellent qualities, was for ever vexing Prothasy, and committing some clumsy awkwardness. Elyas was sure that Hugh had that in him which by-and-by would make his work excellent, and had set his heart upon bringing it out. Was all this hope to end?

Hugh himself was not without thoughts on the subject. The sight of the king, the half smile with which he had been recognised, had stirred up his old desires into ardent longing. Once again nothing in the world seemed so grand as to have the power of fighting, and, if needs were, dying for him. The grave earnest face, saddened by troubles which would have overwhelmed a weaker soul, fired the boy's enthusiasm, where others complained of want of geniality. Then Sir Thomas de Trafford's notice had crimsoned him with pleasure and brought back Dame Edith's sweet face, with which it must be owned Prothasy's could not compare. He was sick of mouldings and ratings, and though the Cathedral always raised a longing in him to be one of the great brotherhood of workers who were making it glorious, he felt at times a dreary conviction that the day would never come, and then the old longing to fling down hammer and chisel grew strong, and he thought that had his father but been there he would surely have yielded to his longing.

Wat was even more excited than he on the matter of this visit, begging hard to be allowed to go with him as far as the palace, and quite content with the prospect of a chance of seeing a squire, or a man-at-arms, or perhaps one of the pages who swaggered about with much contempt for sober citizens. With this hope he stayed outside the palace gate, where a crowd was collected to see the king.

Hugh's heart beat fast, but he went boldly in and asked for John Wakefield. A sturdy, fatherly-looking squire came out, who smiled when he saw so young a visitor, and reported that the knight was in the garden where he had gone to look at the towers of the Cathedral. In parts of the garden the snow lay deep, and the pages had been amusing themselves this morning with building a snow man in one corner, but now were gone off to attend the king, and only Sir Thomas and a chaplain paced the walks. Hugh waited until they turned towards him.

"Who's this?" said the knight stopping. "Beshrew me, but it is the monkey boy, as my little Nell persists in calling him! Knowest thou aught of him, holy father?"

"Naught, gentle sir, more than that by his dress he should be apprenticed to the Masons' Guild—yes, and I have seen him in the Cathedral with Master Gervase."

Beckoned to come nearer, Hugh made his reverence and stood bareheaded, while Sir Thomas questioned him upon what had befallen them: the shipwreck, his father's death, and his present position.

"And thou wouldst sooner chip stones than be in my household? By my faith it seems a strange choice!"

Poor Hugh! It was all he could do to keep the tears back from his eyes.

"I would rather be in your household, sir, than anywhere in the world," he said in a choked voice.

"Sayest thou so?" returned Sir Thomas loudly. "Then, wherefore not? Thy master would do me a favour, I make no doubt, and cancel thy bond, and it would pleasure my little Nell if I took thee and the monkey back with me, though I know not how Wolf would behave. Speak up, without fear, and tell me if thou art willing."

Willing! Every longing in his heart leapt up and cried out to be satisfied. Willing! What would he not give for such a life! It danced up and down before him decked in brightest colours, while on the other side he seemed to hear Franklyn's ceaseless rebukes, and to feel all the weariness of unsuccessful toil. Willing!

But then at that moment his eye fell upon the towers of the Cathedral, and from the building, faint but sweet, there came the sound of young voices chanting the praises of the Lord. And with the sound rushed upon him the remembrance of his father's words, of the promise he had made, of all the wood-carver's hopes, and fears, and longings! Could he disappoint him? He covered his face with his hands and sobbed out, "Noble sir, I would, I would, but I can not!"

"Wherefore?"

"My father—he would have me a carver."

Sir Thomas was silent, but perhaps thinking to pleasure him, the chaplain pushed the matter.

"But thou mayest choose for thyself now that thy father is dead."

"Nay, holy sir," said Hugh, keeping his head down, "but I promised."

"Nevertheless—" began the chaplain, when the knight interrupted.

"Prithee no more, father; a promise is a sacred thing, and the urchin is in the right. Keep covenant is ever the king's word. What was thy promise, boy?"

"That I would learn the craft, and he hoped that in time I might work there," pointing to the Cathedral. "But William Franklyn says I never shall."

"Pay no heed to his croaking," said Sir Thomas heartily. "Work there, ay, that shalt thou, and when I ride here again with the king, thou shalt show me what thou hast done."

He kept the boy longer, speaking kindly, and sending him away at length with the gift of a mark, as he said, to buy a remembrance of Mistress Nell. And when he had gone he turned to the chaplain.

"That was a struggle gallantly got through," he said. "I would I could be sure mine own Edgar would keep as loyally to my words when I am gone. But the boy prince's example and influence are of the worst."

And Hugh?

He had done what was right, but right doing does not always bring immediate satisfaction—very often it is the other way, and we think with regret upon what we have given up, and something within us suggests that we have been too hasty, and that there were ways by which we might have done what was almost right and yet had what we wanted. If Master Gervase could have been brought to consent, knowing all Stephen Bassett's wishes, why, then, surely Hugh might have gone his way, feeling that he had tried to follow his father's road, and only given up when he found he could not get on. And yet twist it as he would, this reasoning would not come fair and smooth, and there was always something which he had to pass over in a hurry. Sir Thomas, too, had said he was right.

Wat pounced upon him before he had gone far, evidently expecting that he would have a great deal to tell—perhaps have seen the king in his crown. At any other time Hugh might have held his peace, but just now there was a hungry longing in his heart, so that he poured all out to Wat—Sir Thomas's offer and his own refusal. It must be owned that he was disappointed that Wat took it as a matter of course, while agreeing that it would have been very fine to have ridden away from Exeter in the king's train.

"Then with Agrippa in thy arms thou might'st have passed for the jester."

"Gramercy for thy fancy," said Hugh offended.

"That would become thee better."

"Ay, it would be rare," answered Wat with a sigh. "I am such an oaf at this stone-cutting that sometimes I could wish myself at the bottom of the sea."

"What made thee take to the craft?"

"To pleasure my old mother. She is a cousin of Franklyn's, and thought I was a made man when she had stinted herself sufficiently to pay the premium. But I shall never be more than a mason," added Wat dolefully. "Now thou hast it in thee."

"I know not. Franklyn has never a good word for aught I do."

"Never heed old Franklyn. He is as sour as a crab, because he wanted the master to take his little jackanapes of a nephew as prentice. He would like to keep thee back, but do thou hold on and all will come right. Why, even I can see what thy work is like, and so does he, and so does the master, only the master will do nothing to touch Franklyn's authority, and so he holds his peace."

"But you think he knows?" asked Hugh eagerly.

"Think? How should he not know? He can measure us all better than Franklyn, and he knows, too, that I am more fitted for a life in the greenwood than to be chopping away with mallet and chisel."

It was very unusual for Wat to talk with so much shrewdness and common sense. Usually he was addle-pated enough, caring little for ratings, and plunging into trouble with the most good-natured tactlessness, so that friends and foes alike showered abuse upon him. Hugh had taken it for granted that he would be the same wherever he was, never realising that his present life was especially distasteful to him, and yet that he accepted it without gainsaying. It gave his words now a weight which was quite unusual, for he seemed never to suppose it possible that Hugh could go against his promise to his father, while he quite acknowledged that the other life would have been delightful. All seemed to arrange itself simply into two sides, right and wrong, so that Hugh began to wonder how he could ever have doubted when it was so clear to Wat.

In the house he found Joan shrieking because her father could not take her forth, and he was glad enough to make her over to Hugh, telling him that the king was to ride down the High Street to see the new bridge before returning to the banquet at the Guildhall, and warning him to take care not to allow Joan to be over-much entangled in the crowd. Then he put his hands on the boy's shoulders and looked into his face.

"What said the knight to thee?"

"He offered, if thou wouldst consent, sir, to take me back with him, and to bring me up in his household."

"As I expected," said Elyas, gravely. "And that would content thee?"

"It is what I ever longed for," said poor Hugh.

There was a pause. Gervase seemed to find it difficult to put the next question.

"Does the knight come here then to see me?"

"Nay," said the boy wearily, "it were no use, goodman. I told him that I was bound by my promise to my father."

"Ay, didst thou so? And what said he?"

"There was a holy father there who would have urged me, but the knight stopped him, and said a promise was binding, and that the king's word was ever 'Keep covenant.'"

Gervase's eyes glistened. "It was well, it was well. Hadst thou been set upon it, Hugh, I had not withstood thee, but I should have grieved. No blessing comes from self-seeking. And hast thou," he added more cheerily, "hast thou forgotten the corbels thou hast to do for the bishop?"

His words put fresh heart into the boy, and he felt that even had he followed his own longings it would have cost him much to leave Master Gervase. Then Joan ran in, warmly and daintily dressed, gathering up her little skirts to show Hugh her new long pointed shoes, all her tears forgotten, and her mind running upon the king and his knights. Her mother, though sharp with Hugh, would trust her little maid anywhere with him, and the two set forth down the narrow streets where was a throng of villeins, of country people who had poured in for miles round, of guild-brothers in their distinctive dresses, of monks from the monasteries of Saint Nicholas and Saint James, grey and black friars, Kalendar sisters, while mingling with these graver dresses were the more brilliantly clad retainers of the nobles who had accompanied or come to meet the king, most gorgeous among whom were those of the household of Dame Alicia de Mohun, who had journeyed in great state from Tor Mohun, near Torbay, and the trappings of whose palfrey caused the citizens much amazement. As many minstrels, dancing girls, and jongleurs had collected as if it had been fair time, and the bakers who sold bread by the Carfax were so pressed upon that they were forced to gather up their goods and remove them hastily.

Joan did not find it as delightful as she expected. Not all Hugh's efforts could keep the crowd from pressing upon her, and he looked anxiously about for some safer means of letting her see the show. He spied at last a projection from one of the houses where he thought she might stand, and from whence she could look over the shoulders of the crowd, and there with much difficulty and pushing he managed to place her, standing himself so that he could both shield and hold her. There was no chance of seeing anything himself, for he was hedged in by a moving crowd, and more than one looked rather angrily upon him for having secured this standing-point before they had discovered its advantages. But Joan was mightily pleased. She was out of the press, and could see all that was to be seen, upon which she chattered volubly to her faithful guard below.

They had long to wait, but there was enough amusement for her not to weary, and when at last she became a little silent and Hugh wondered whether she would be content much longer, a cry of "The king!" was raised, and heads were eagerly stretched to see him turn out from Broad Gate. Down came the gay train, larger than that of the day before, owing to the many nobles and knights, Champernownes, Chudleighs, Fulfords, Pomeroys, Courtenays, and others, who had come into the city, and very noble they looked turning down the steep hill between the old houses.

But Hugh could neither see nor think of them, he was in so much dread that Joan would be swept or dragged off her standing place. The people were wild to have sight of the king, and those who were behind looked covetously at the projection. One or two pressed violently by Hugh, muttering that children were best left at home, and at last, as the cavalcade drew nearer and the excitement heightened, a wizened little man pushed the girl off and would have clambered into the place if a stronger fellow had not collared him and climbed there himself. Joan meanwhile was in danger of being trampled under foot, though Hugh fought and kicked with all the vigour in the world, shielding her at the cost of many hard blows on himself from those who were bent only upon pushing forward without heeding what was in their way. Joan, however, was not one to be maltreated without protest, and the instant she realised what had happened, she uttered a series of piercing shrieks, which caused the king and his train to look in her direction. Edward pulled up, and two or three of the men-at-arms, hastily parting the crowd, disclosed Joan clinging to Hugh, uttering woeful cries and prayers to be taken home. One of them would have raised her in his arms, but this was fresh terror, and whispering to Hugh, "Bring her thyself," he pushed them gently along towards the royal party.

"Is the child hurt?" asked Edward hastily, and then recognising Hugh, who was red with shame at his own plight, and to have Joan hanging round his neck, the king smiled, and beckoned to him. Hugh bent on his knee as well as he could for Joan, and answered the king's brief questions clearly. Someone had pulled the little maid down, and she was afraid of being trampled upon, and Joan, convinced now that she was in safety, relaxed her hold and gazed from one to the other with eyes full of innocent awe.

"She is a fair little maiden," said Edward, kindly, "and thou art a brave prentice. Ever keep on the side of the weak. Now, my lords," he added, "as the matter is not serious, we will ride to the bridge."

The people cheered lustily as he passed on, and Hugh and Joan were the hero and heroine of the hour.

"What said he? What said he?"

"Blessings on him, he hath a kindly heart! There's many a proud baron would have paid no heed to a babe's cries, but I warrant me he thinks of his lady."

"Where's the churl that pushed her off? A good ducking should he have."

But, fearing this turn of the tide, the man had slunk away, and Joan, pleased as she was with the admiring epithets bestowed upon her, desired to be taken home, and made a discovery which moved her to tears, in the fact that the long toes of her new shoes, subjects of much pride, were hopelessly-ruined.

She reached the house weeping, and her mother, flying out, rated Hugh soundly before hearing anything of what had happened, whereupon Joan flung her arms round his neck, said that Hugh was good, the king had said so, and the people were naughty. Prothasy listening in amazement could scarce believe her ears, making Hugh tell his story over and over again, and pouring it out to Elyas when he came back from the banquet.

"The king called her a fair maiden, what thinkest thou of that, goodman?" she asked proudly.

"And Hugh a brave prentice, what thinkest thou of that, goodwife?" returned her husband, with a smile.

Chapter Eleven.

Agrippa Brings Promotion.

The king's visit was short, for the next day he departed, and Hugh with a swelling heart saw Sir Thomas ride away, and with him all chance of changing his condition. Still, he had got over the first pangs, was more content, and resolved that, whatever Franklyn might do, he would not be discouraged. He made another resolve. As has been said, the apprentices had plenty of holidays, and Hugh cared nothing for the cock-fighting, which was a favourite amusement. He liked football better, but he made up his mind that some of his holiday time should be spent in a stone carving of Agrippa. If it pleased Master Gervase,—why, then, his hopes flew high.

He worked hard at his design, keeping it jealously hid from all but Wat, whom he would have found it difficult to shut out, and who was profoundly impressed by his ambition. Agrippa was not the easiest of models, since to keep still was an impossibility, but Hugh managed to get him into clay very fairly, and in a good position. He was dreadfully disheartened when he tried to reproduce it in stone; it fell far short of his conception, and appeared to him to be lifeless. Indeed, had it not been for Wat, he might have given up his attempt in despair; but Wat's interest was intense, and he was never weary of foretelling what Master Gervase would say of it, and how even Franklyn might be compelled to admire in spite of grudging. How this might have been, it is impossible to say; Hugh was spared from making the trial, for, as it happened, just when Lent began Franklyn was seized with severe rheumatic pains, which made it impossible for him to work, or even come to the yard. Generally one of the other journeymen on such an emergency stepped into his place, but this time, for some reason or other, Master Gervase overlooked things himself. He made a very careful examination, and, for almost the first time in his life, Wat received actual praise.

"Thou hast got a notion into thy head at last."

Wat could not resist making a face expressive of his amazement.

"'Twas thou hammered it there," he whispered to Hugh. "If I tell the gammer she will think all her prophecies are coming true. Now where's thy work? Hast stuck it where he must needs see?"

"Ay, see a failure," said Hugh, dolefully.

But Wat was too intent upon watching Elyas to have an ear for these misgivings of the artist. He fidgeted about instead of working, and got a sharp rebuke from the master for wasting his time; indeed, Gervase was so much taken up with seeing that the right vein of the Purbeck quarry was being used for carrying on the delicate arcades of the triforium, that it was long before he left the men engaged upon it and came to Hugh. His eye fell immediately upon the little figure.

"When didst thou this?" he demanded, taking it up.

"In holiday time, goodman."

Long and silently the master examined it, and every moment Hugh's fluttering hopes sank lower. He was sure it had never looked so ill before. At last Elyas raised his head.

"It doth credit to thine age," he said, warmly. "Faults there are, no doubt: the head a little larger than it should be except in fashioning the grotesque; the space across the forehead too broad. But what pleases me is that thou heist caught the character of the creature, thine eye having reported it to thee faithfully. If Franklyn saw it he would own," he added, raising his voice so that all might hear, "that thou hadst earned advancement. Finish this moulding, and I will set thee on some small bosses which Dame Alicia de Mohun hath commanded for her private chapel, and if thou wilt thou mayest work Agrippa into one of them."

If Hugh were pleased, Elyas was hardly less so. He had been greatly desirous to find some excuse by which, without seeming to set aside Franklyn's rule, he might give the boy a chance which he considered he well deserved. He had understood something of Hugh's feelings when the hopes he had given up were once more dangled before his longing eyes, and the kindly master longed for an opportunity of encouraging him in his present work. The carving of the monkey was clever enough to have really surprised him. Franklyn's illness came at an excellent time, and no one could complain of favouritism. So he thought Oddly enough, the only one who did was Roger, the elder prentice, who had hitherto seemed quite indifferent. He was manifestly out of temper, muttering that it was enough to have the beast jabbering at you in life, without having him stuck up in stone, and for the first time doing his best in the small room the three apprentices shared to make things bad for Hugh. But Hugh was much too proud and happy to care for this, and he had Wat on his side, so that Roger's enmity could not do much. Wat's great desire was to be himself perpetuated as a grinning mask in the centre of a boss. He was for ever making horrible faces in order that Hugh might judge whether they were not grotesque enough, and poor little Joan, coming upon him one day with a mouth as it seemed to her stretching from ear to ear, and goggle saucer eyes, was so frightened that it was all the boys could do to quiet her.

"If only I could round my eyes and yet frown fearfully!" cried Wat, making ineffectual struggles to carry out his aspiration. "There, is that better? What do I look like now?"

"Like a grinning cat," said Hugh, bursting into a laugh.

"Not a demon? Perchance if I squinted?"

"Hearken, Wat, I will not spoil my bosses by such an ill-favoured countenance, but the very first gargoyle the master sets me to make, thou shalt be my model. That is a pact."

"I shall?"

"Ay, truly."

"I will practise the most fearsome faces," cried Wat, joyfully. "There shall be no such gargoyle for miles around! Where do you think it will be placed? There is a talk of a new Guildhall in the High Street, and it would be fine to stare down and grin at the citizens. Then, whenever he saw it, it would remind the master of Prentice Wat. Art thou coming out on Refreshment Sunday?"

"Where?"

"I never saw such a boy as thou, thou knowest naught! Why, we make a figure of straw—Hugh, you could make it finely!"

"What to represent?"

"Nay, I know not—oh, ay, I remember me, it is Winter, only the country people will have it 'tis Death, 'tis so gruesome and grisly, and they hate to have us bring it to their houses, and give us cakes to keep it away. A party of us are going as far as Topsham and Clyst this time. Wilt come?"

"'Tis naught but mumming!"

Nevertheless Hugh consented to shape the figure, which represented Winter in the last stage of decrepitude, and Wat begged an old tattered cloak and hood, so that it really gave not a bad idea of a tottering old man, when about twenty apprentices, sinking their constant rivalries, set out in high glee to visit the neighbouring hamlets, and, when all was done, burn Winter in the meadows outside the walls, Agrippa, by common consent, of the party.

They had great merriment, though not by any means universal welcome, for some of the country folk were so frightened that they closed the doors of their huts, and stuffed up the window lest the hateful thing should be thrust in that way. Others, seeing them in the distance, ran out with cakes and spiced ale, and even pennies, begging them to come no nearer. The boys were very scornful of such fears.

"What harm could it bring thee, goody?"

"Alack, alack, young sirs, I know not, but this I know, that come last March Snell the smith would have it into his house, and before the year was out, the goodwife, who had been ailing for years, and never died before, was a corpse. Here's as good a simnel cake as you will find for miles round, and welcome, but, prithee, bring the thing no nearer."

Others there were, however, who made the boys welcome, and feasted them so bountifully that Hugh vowed he had never eaten so much in his life, and Agrippa grew to treat his dainties with scorn. They took their way at length back to the meadows, bestowed the cloak and hood upon a blind beggar, who, guessing what was going on, besought the charity of a few rags, and built a grand bonfire, on the top of which Winter was seated, in order, as they said, that he might be warm for once. There were other groups of the same sort scattered about the fields, and many elders had ridden out to see the fun, which reminded them of their own boyish days. Joan was perched in front of her father on the broad-backed grey, insisting upon keeping as near to Hugh's bonfire as the grey could be induced to go, and crying out with delight as the tongues of fire leapt up, and the brushwood crackled, and at last, old Winter's straw being reached, a tall and glorious pyramid of fire rushed upwards; the lads shouted, and the reign of Winter was held to be ended.

Before Lent finished, Franklyn hobbled back to the yard. Hugh expected that he would have been very angry at finding him put to really advanced work, but it is possible that Franklyn was himself not sorry that things had changed without his having had to give way. He muttered gruffly that the boy was no wonder, but had improved with teaching; and he showed no spite, for though always strict with Hugh, he took pains to correct his faults carefully, so that his training was thoroughly good, and Gervase was well satisfied with the two bosses which were Hugh's share of Dame Alicia's work. Agrippa peeped from one, half concealed by foliage, and the other was formed of ivy and holly. When summer came he was resolved to follow the master's advice and study different plants and leaves, so as to catch the beautiful free natural curves. He had grown to love his work dearly, and to have high hopes about it, but perhaps it was the recollection of his father's last words, at a time when visions of earthly fame seemed dim and worthless, which kept him from thinking only, as Roger thought, of his own advancement and glory, and ever held before him, as the crown of his work, the hope some day to give of his best for the House of the Lord.

The bishop had not forgotten him, often asking Master Gervase for the little prentice who meant to carve one of the corbels.

"*Ay*, my lord, and it would not greatly surprise me if he carried out his thought," said Elyas, with a smile. And he told the bishop of his work for Dame Alicia's chantry. "He hath a marvellous fancy for his age," he added.

"Brother Ambrose at the Kalendarhay complains that he is idle, but says he can do anything with his fingers," remarked the bishop. "He would fain he were a monk, that he might paint in the missals, but thou and I would have him do nobler work. Not that I would say aught against the good brothers," he added, rapidly crossing himself. "Everyone to his calling, and the boy's lies not between their walls. Keep him to it, keep him to it, goodman; give him a thorough training, for which none is better fitted than thyself. It is my earnest desire that proper workers may be trained to give their best in this building, as of old the best was given for the Temple. Thou and I may never see the fruit of our labours—what of that? One soweth and another reapeth, and so it is for the glory of God, let that suffice. The walls of the choir go on well, methinks, and in another year or two we shall have reached the Lady Chapel."

"Ay, my lord."

"And then there must be no more work done by thee for town or country. I claim it all. So thou hadst best finish off Dame Alicia's chantry."

"No fear, my lord. The lady is impatient, and will not tarry till then. I shall have to go down in the summer to see after the fixing of these bosses, and of some other work which she hath confided to me, and that will end it."

The good bishop, indeed, was inclined to be jealous over anything which took away Gervase's time and attention, and the stone mason had some difficulty in keeping his own hands free, his skill being of great repute among all the gentlemen round, and some of them being of fiery dispositions, ill-disposed to brook waiting. There was plenty doing in the yard, and often visitors to see how the work got on or to give orders, and, as Hugh was the only one in the house who could write or read, his master frequently called him to his aid when a scroll was brought from some neighbouring abbot or prior.

At Easter they had, as usual, the gammon of bacon, to show widespread hatred of the Jews, and the tansy pudding in remembrance of the bitter herbs. Also another old custom there was, the expectation of which kept Gervase on the watch with a comical look on his face, and set Joan quivering with excitement for, as she confided to Hugh in a very loud whisper, mother had promised that she should be by "to see father heaved."

She was terribly disappointed when he went out, and scarcely consoled by his taking her with him, and when at last he brought her home, clasping a great bunch of primroses in her little hot hands, she was not to be separated from him.

"Why dost thou not go and look for thy friend Hugh?"

"They might come and do it."

"Perhaps I shall slip away and not let them find me at all."

But the bare idea of this produced so much dismay, that Elyas was obliged to hasten to assure her that he would not resort to any such underhand proceeding. He turned to Prothasy with a smile.

"An I am to endure it, I would the silly play were over."

"Thou wilt not escape, goodman. Master Allen, the new warden of the Tuckers' Guild, has had such a lifting that he was fain to give twelve pennies to be set down again."

"They'll not get twelve pennies from me. Richard Allen is an atomy of a man."

"Ay, thy broad shoulders will make it a different matter," said Prothasy, looking proudly at him; "but be not over-confident, goodman, for King Edward is a bigger man than thou, and they heaved him one Easter till he cried for mercy and offered ransom."

Nothing more was heard till supper-time, when, as Elyas sat at the head of his table, four stout girls rushed into the room, and, amid loud laughter from everyone and ecstatic shrieks and clappings from Joan, lifted the rough stool on which he was seated into the air, and swung him backwards and forwards.

"There, there, ye foolish wenches! I'm too heavy a load. Put me down, and the goodwife shall give ye your cakes."

"Twelve pennies, goodman! Thou, a new warden, wouldst not pay less than Richard Allen of the Tuckers?"

"Ay, would I though."

Whereupon he was screamed at and rocked as unmercifully as any boat in a storm, until between laughter and vexation he promised all that they asked, and the four girls went away declaring their arms would ache for a week.

"Ye will not be able to make the dumb cake on Saint Mark's Eve," Gervase called after them, "and then, no chance for you to see your sweethearts at midnight."

"No need for that, goodman," answered the eldest and prettiest, "we know who they are already."

So many holidays fell at that fair time of the year that the master grumbled his work would ne'er be done.

"May Day come and gone, ye shall have no more."

But May Day itself could not be slighted, for long before sunrise the lads and lasses were out to gather May, or any greenery that might be got, and the prentices tramped through mud and mire, and charged the thickets of dense brushwood valiantly. Wat was covered with scratches, and a sorry object as they trudged home by sunrise, in order to decorate the house door with branches, and all the other boys and girls were at the same work, so that in a short time the street looked a very bower of May.

And now the days growing longer and the country drier, there was less danger from travelling, and a general desire in everyone's heart to be doing something or going somewhere, or otherwise proving themselves to have some part in this world, which never looks so fair or so hopeful as at the beautiful spring season. Many of the neighbouring gentry rode into the city, and the ladies were glad to wear their whimsically scalloped garments, and their fine mantles, and to display their tight lacing in the streets instead of country lanes, as well as to visit the clothiers and drapers for a fresh supply; while their lords took the opportunity of looking at horses, playing at tennis, and some times, when much in want of ready money, disposing of a charter of liberties, to gain which the citizens were ready to pay a heavy fine.

Master Gervase had many visits from these lords and knights, and more work pressed upon him than he would undertake. My Lord of Devon had pretty well insisted upon his carrying out some change in his house at Exminster, where some forty years later was born William Courtenay, the future Archbishop of Canterbury, and Gervase was one day cutting the notches in a wooden tally, made of a slip of willow—which was the manner of giving a receipt—and handing it to the bailiff, when a tall man holding a little girl by the hand strode into the yard.

"It is Sir Hereward Hamlin," Wat whispered to Hugh.

Sir Hereward Hamlin, it appeared, had a commission which he would entrust to none but Elyas, and very wroth he became when he found it could not be undertaken. It was evident that he was not used to be gainsaid, for he stormed and tried to browbeat the stonemason, who showed no signs of disturbance. The little girl also listened quite unmoved.

"They say she is as proud as he is," Wat the gossip commented under his breath, "for all her name is Dulcia; and the poor lady her mother scarce can call her soul her own between them."

"I hope the master will not yield," muttered Hugh indignantly.

There was small fear of that. Sir Hereward's fiery temper and passionate outbreaks had caused him to be much disliked in the city, and Gervase would at no time have been disposed to work for him even had time been at his disposal.

"It is impossible, your worship," he said coldly, nor could anything turn his resolution, so that Sir Hereward had to leave, muttering angry maledictions upon upstart knaves who know not how to order themselves to their betters.

"I would he knew how to order himself to his own," said Gervase to Franklyn, "but he has never been friendly to the king since he was forced to restore the crown lands and divers of our rights which his fathers had illegally seized. If I had yielded and done his work he would have thought the honour sufficient payment."

When the week of rogations was at an end, with its processions and singing of litanies all about the streets from gate to gate, Gervase told Hugh of a plan which mightily delighted him, for it was none other but to take him with him on his journey to Tor Brewer, or Tor Mohun, where he had to go on this business of the Dame Alicia's chantry. She had already sent serfs and horses to fetch the carved work, and with them an urgent message for Master Gervase to come; and as Hugh had done his work well—marvellously well, Elyas privately thought—he determined to give him the delight of seeing it fixed in its place, and the two set off together one morning in early June, with Joan kissing her hand from the balcony. The only pang to Hugh was the leaving Agrippa, but Wat was his devoted slave, and solemnly vowed not to neglect him, and, moreover, to protect him from Roger, who had developed a keen dislike for the creature, while Mistress Prothasy had quite forgotten hers.

It was a fair morning, and the country, then far more thickly wooded than now, was in its loveliest dress of dainty green. The brushwood was full of birds, thrushes and blackbirds drowning the smaller notes by the jubilance of their whistling, while, high up, the larks were pouring out a rapturous flood of song. It was the same road along which Hugh had journeyed twice before, but how different it looked now, and how strange it seemed to him that he should ever have run away from the home where he was so happy! Something of the same thought may have been in Gervase's mind, for when they were not very far from Exminster, riding between banks, and under oaks, of which the yellow leaf was not yet fully out, he pointed to a spot in the hedge, and said with a smile:

"'Twas there I found thee, Hugh, and a woe begone object thou wast!" Then, as he saw the boy redden, he went on kindly, "But that is all over and done with long ago, and now thou art content, if I mistake not."

"More than content, good sir."

"That is well, that is well. A little patience will often carry us through the darkest days. By-and-by show me about where thou wast wrecked. Ay, the sea is a terrible place for mischances, and for myself I cannot think how men can be found willing to encounter such risks. There is talk of building larger vessels and adventuring longer voyages, but 'tis a rash idea. What know we of the awful regions that they might light upon, or whether the vessels might not be carried too close to the edge of the world? Nay, nay, keep to land, say I. Those who must explore may travel there as Marco Polo hath done, and indeed there are many tales going about the wonders of the Court of the great Khan of Tartary."

The road, as they journeyed on, became very beautiful, so wooded was it and broken, and with ever-widening views of water to the left, while on the right after a time they saw the ridges of Dartmoor, a very bleak and barren country, as Elyas told the boy, but now looking softly grey and delicate in colour. By this time they had reached the Teign, and here at Kingsteignton stopped to rest their horses, at a house belonging to the Burdons of that place, Elyas having done some work for them, and requiring to see it in its finished condition. Plain country people they were, and awkward and uncouth in manners, two or three boys on bare-backed colts riding up as Gervase and Hugh arrived, and pointing at them with bursts of laughter. The girls, Hugh thought, were little better, and the fashion of their garments curiously odd and slatternly. When supper—which was very plentifully provided—was over, they set forth again on their journey, getting into a most vile road, which lasted for some miles, but took them without adventure to Tor Mohun, although it led them through an extraordinary number of rocks and tors, and also between exceedingly thick woods.

Gervase had never been there before, and was no more prepared than Hugh for the view which met their eyes when they came out of the circle of these woods. For there lay a very noble bay, well shut in, and with very beautiful and thickly wooded cliffs rising up on the eastern side. In a hollow of these cliffs and hills there clustered a few miserable hovels, otherwise it was a wild solitude, only so tempered by a kindly climate and the softness of the sea breezes that there was nothing rough or savage about it; and just now, towards sunset, with the sea like opal glass, and the colours all most bright and yet delicate, and the thorns yet in blossom, it was exceedingly pleasant to the eye, and Dame Alicia's house, though standing back, had it well in view.

It was plain that she was a great lady by the size of the building and the number of retainers about, but they heard afterwards that these were not all hers, Sir William de Sandridge from Stoke Gabriel, and Sir Robert le Denys of Blagdon in the moor, having ridden over to spend two or three nights. An elderly squire took charge of Gervase and his apprentice, showing them the little room that was to be theirs, and telling the warden that his lady had been eagerly expecting his coming, and would see him the next day.

Elyas asked whether he should find workmen in the chapel early in the morning.

"No fear, goodman," said the squire with a laugh; "Dame Alicia is not one to let the grass grow under her feet, and I would not answer but what she may keep them there all night. Go as early as thou wilt; follow this passage, turn down another to the right, and thou wilt come to a door with steps, which will take thee there."

The next few days were days of both wonder and amusement to Hugh. Dame Alicia was a fiery and impetuous little lady, using such strong language as would have brought her a heavy fine had she been an apprentice; ruling her household and serfs with much sharpness, disposed to domineer, yet with a kind heart which prevented any serious tyranny, and sometimes moved her to shame for too hasty acts. She was at times very impatient with Elyas, expecting her wishes to be carried out in an unreasonably short time, and that all other work should give way to hers; but the stonemason had a dignity of his own, which never failed him, and kept him quietly resolute in spite of sudden storms. He would not consent to undertake the carving of the pulpit, or ambo, which she wanted set about, declaring that he had too much already on hand, nor would he yield to Sir Robert le Denys and go to Blagdon to advise on alterations there. All, however, that he had to do at Tor Mohun he did admirably. It was a proud day to Hugh when he saw the bosses he had carved fixed in the vaulted roof. He worked all day in the chantry with delight, and would scarcely have left it had not Gervase insisted on his going forth into the air. Then sometimes he would go out in one of the rude fishing-boats, and was delighted to find a man who knew Andrew of Dartmouth, and promised to convey tidings of Hugh to him.

At the end of a week, in spite of Dame Alicia's reluctance, Elyas and Hugh went back to Exeter again, and to the old life, which had become so familiar.

Chapter Twelve.

With the Prentices in the Meadows.

Time passed on, weeks, months, years: slowly, though happily, for the children; ever faster and faster for the elders. Joan was still the only child, the darling of the house, but with a sweet, frank nature which was proof against spoiling. Roger had long finished his seven years' apprenticeship, and now worked by the day as journeyman; even Wat was close on the end of his term, but nobody seemed to think he could ever be anything except Prentice Wat, whom everybody laughed at and everybody liked, even better than they knew. Nevertheless, by dint of hard belabouring of brains, and a most impatient patience, for he was ever rating him for his dulness, and yet never giving up the teaching, Hugh had managed to hammer more out of Wat than had been supposed possible in the beginning of things. It was very hard to get him to take in an idea, but once in his head, he sometimes showed an aptitude for working it out which surprised the others, and caused Hugh delightful moments of triumph.

As for Hugh himself, his progress was astonishing. If he still lacked something of the technical skill of Franklyn, there was no one, except Gervase himself, who could come near his power of design. The boy had an intense love of nature, nothing was lost upon him. When he was in the fields or woods, he would note the exquisite curve of branches, the uncurling of ferns, the spring of grass or rushes, and was for ever trying to reproduce them. By this means his eye and hand were trained in the very best school, and his designs had an extraordinary beauty and freedom of line, devoid of all stiffness and conventionality. He could never be induced to delight in the grinning masks and monsters which were the joy of Wat's soul, but when any delicate and dainty work was called for, it was always Hugh who was set to do it.

His pride and delight in the Cathedral was scarcely less than the bishop's. Bishop Bitton was steadily carrying out his work in the choir, so as to complete the design of his predecessors. The choir was now entirely rebuilt, and united to the Lady Chapel, left standing at the end. The beautiful vaulting of the roof was in course of construction, and pushed on with all the speed that good work would allow. For one characteristic of the work of those days was that it was of the best. There was no competition, which we are accustomed to look upon as an actual necessity, but in place of this the guilds, which controlled labour and held it in their own hands, exercised a very strict oversight upon materials and execution, so that nothing which was bad or indifferent was allowed to pass; there was no possibility of underselling, nor of the workman being underpaid.

The bishop had by no means forgotten his idea about the corbels. As the beautiful clustered shafts of the columns—of soft grey unpolished Purbeck marble—were raised to support the arches, above each one was built in the long shapeless block, waiting to be some day carved into shape. Gervase, also, was fired into enthusiasm when he spoke of them, and if Gervase, then yet more Hugh. Much of his handiwork was already to be found in the Cathedral, but this was of more importance, and there was even talk of the guild admitting into their number a skilled workman from France, famous for his skill in stone carving.

One day, in the June of 1302, master and apprentice were standing in the choir, Hugh having just come down from work on the triforium.

"I find my eye ever running over those blocks," said Elyas with a smile, "and picturing them as they might look, finished. To-day, at any rate, I have brought one question to an end."

"What, goodman?"

"I shall be offered my choice of which to work upon myself."

"Ay?" said Hugh eagerly.

"I shall choose that," he said, pointing to one about half-way between the entrance of the choir and the spot where it was designed that the bishop's seat should be. "There is something friendly and inviting in that pillar, it fits in with my design. Thou, Hugh, must take whichever they offer thee."

"If they will accept me at all!"

"I think so," said Elyas gravely. "'Tis true thy lack of years is against thee, but there is no other hindrance, and I believe they will trust me in the matter. How old art thou now, Hugh?"

"Just seventeen, sir."

"Already? But, yes, it must be so. It is all but six years since I stumbled upon thee in the street, a little fellow, no older than our Joan is now. Much has happened in the kingdom since then, but here the time has flown peacefully."

Much, indeed, had happened to weight the last years of the reign of the great king. The second war in Scotland was over; Edward had married again, the Princess Margaret of France being his chosen wife. Parliaments had by his efforts become more frequent and more important, and the parliament of Lincoln, in 1301, marked an era in representative government, when one hundred and thirty seven cities and boroughs sent up representatives. Archbishop Winchelsey was still trying to enforce the papal supremacy, which Edward ever resisted, and certain disaffected nobles joined the archbishop. The king dealt with the two principal conspirators, Norfolk and Hereford, both firmly and leniently. Winchelsey he would not himself judge, but his ambassador placed the matter in the hands of the pontiff, who immediately cited the archbishop to Rome, to answer for his conduct. William Thorn, a monk of Canterbury, thus describes the next scene: "When the archbishop knew that he was thus cited, he went to the king to ask for permission to cross the sea. And when the king heard of his coming, he ordered the doors of his presence chamber to be thrown open, that all who wished might enter, and hear the words which he should address to him. And having heard the archbishop, he thus replied to him:—'The permission to cross the sea which you ask of us we willingly grant you—but permission to return grant we none:—bearing in mind your treachery, and the treason which at our parliament at Lincoln you plotted against us;—whereof a letter under your seal is witness, and plainly testifies against you. We leave it to the pope to avenge our wrongs; and as you have deserved, so shall he recompense you. But from our favour and mercy, which you ask, we utterly exclude you; because merciless you have yourself been, and therefore deserve not to obtain mercy.' And so we part with Winchelsey." (*The Greatest of all the Plantagenets.*)

At Exeter, however, as Gervase said, the time had passed peaceably. Two burgesses had indeed with much pain and trouble journeyed all the way to Lincoln, and came back with marvellous stories of the magnificence of the barons, the crowds of retainers, the quantity of provisions supplied, and the deliciousness of sea-wolves, now tasted for the first time.

And, greatly to Hugh's delight, it appeared that Sir Thomas de Trafford, being there with his lady and children, applied to one of the Exeter burgesses for news of Hugh, and sent word he was glad to hear that he was a good lad, and doing credit to his craft. And Dame Edith despatched him a token, a rosary from the Holy Land, and the two sisters a gift of a mark to Agrippa, to buy him cakes.

On poor Agrippa the years had, perhaps, told the most hardly. He suffered much from the cold winters, and had lost a good deal of his activity. But on the whole he had a very happy life, with no fear of ill-usage from boy or man, for he was as well-known to all the citizens as any other dweller in the High Street, and was held to be under the special protection of the guild of which Elyas was warden.

That June in which Gervase and Hugh talked in the Cathedral found Wat in low spirits. He had been out of his apprenticeship for nearly a year, but this was the first midsummer that had fallen since he had been promoted to what might be called man's estate, which promised to require more sacrifices to its dignity than he was at all willing to make. On one point he had besought Master Gervase so piteously that the master had yielded, and allowed him to remain in the house. Another apprentice, one Hal Crocker, had been admitted, and of him Wat was absurdly jealous, so that Hugh sometimes had to interfere, though Hal was a malapert boy, very well able to take care of himself.

But Midsummer Eve had ever been a time of high revel for the prentices.

"And this year the bonfires will be bigger than ever," cried Wat in a tragic voice. "Alack, why couldn't the master keep me on as a prentice?"

"What an oaf thou art!"

"I care not for being an oaf, but I hate to be a journeyman, and have no merriment."

Poor Wat! He did not so much mind giving up what Hugh liked best in all the day, the wreathing the doorways with fennel, green birch, and lilies, but to lose the joy of collecting the brushwood and piling it in great heaps, with much rivalry among the lads as to which was the highest and best built—this was indeed doleful. The meadows were thronged with crowds, among which he wandered disconsolate, giving sly help when he could do so without loss of dignity, until to his great joy he espied Gervase himself dragging a great bush to one of the heaps, upon which, with a shout of delight, Wat flung himself into a thorny thicket, and emerged with as much as his arms could clasp.

Meanwhile other things besides fuel were being brought into the field by goodwives and serving maids. Round each bonfire were placed tables on which supper was bountifully spread, and when it grew dusk and the fires were lighted, all passers-by were invited to eat, besides the friends of the providers. The whole scene was extremely gay and brilliant, and between crackling of green things and chatter of many voices, the noise was prodigious. Wat was by this time as happy as a king, running here and there as freely as ever in prentice days, helping the smaller boys, seeing that there was no lack of provisions, and inexhaustible in his good humour.

Several of Master Gervase's friends were seated at his tables, and among them one Master Tirell, a member of the Goldsmiths' Guild, with his wife and daughters. Hugh had noticed one of these as a very fair and dainty little damsel in a pale blue kirtle, who seemed somewhat shy and frightened, and kept very close to her mother's side. The merriment, indeed, grew somewhat boisterous as the darkness crept on, and the bonfires were constantly fed with fresh fuel, and certain of the younger of the prentices amused themselves by dragging out burning brands, and pursuing each other with shrieks of excitement about the meadows. Foremost among these was Hal Crocker, who managed more than once to slip by Wat before the elder lad could seize him, and whose wild spirits led him to fling about the burning sticks which he pulled out, to the danger of the bystanders. Suddenly, after one of these wild rushes there was a cry of terror. Thomasin Tirell, the fair-haired girl already mentioned, started up and ran wildly forwards, stretching out her hands, and screaming for help. Almost before the others could realise what had happened, Wat had sprung towards her, thrown her on the grass, and pressed out the fire with his hands. She was scarcely hurt at all, though sorely frightened, bursting into sobs and hiding her face on her mother's shoulder as soon as she was on her feet again, and trembling like a terrified bird. Her mother soothed her, while Master Tirell heartily thanked Wat, and Gervase looked angrily round in search of the culprit.

"Beshrew me, but it was bravely done, and thou art a gallant lad," said Master Tirell, a portly, red-faced man; "St. Loys shall have a silver chain for this, for the poor silly maid might have been in a sorry plight had she run much farther, and the fire been fanned into flame. Shake hands—what, are thy hands so burned? See here, goodwife, here is room for thy leechcraft."

It was in vain that Wat protested, he was forced to display his hands, at which Thomasin gazed, horror-struck, with tears running over her blue eyes, and hands clasped on her breast. In fact, Wat was suddenly elevated into quite a new position, that of a hero, for the citizens pressed to the spot from all sides and heaped praises upon him.

"'Twas nothing!" he kept saying awkwardly, turning redder and redder at each congratulation, and looking from side to side for a loophole of

escape. Then, as Hugh came rushing up with an eager "What is it?"—
"That mischievous loon Hal! If I can but lay hands on him!"

"Hath he set anyone on fire?"

"Ay, young Mistress Tirell. Nay, mistress, prithee think not of it—my
hands will be well to-morrow—'tis nothing, Mistress Thomasin—
Hugh," (aside), "get me out of this, for I never felt such a fool!"

But there was no escape for Wat. Hal, having been caught, and
received summary punishment from his master, was sent home, and
the party sat down again, some to go on with Prothasy's good things,
and Thomasin to recover a little from her condition. Nothing would
serve but that Wat must sit down, too, between Thomasin and her
elder sister, Alice, and there he was more confused than ever by
faltered thanks, and grateful glances of the blue eyes.

"How was it?" asked Alice, whispering across him.

"Alack, I know not!" said the other girl, shuddering. "I felt something
hot under my elbow, and looked down, and there was a line of flame
darting up, and then I screamed, and then—" to Wat—"you came."

"I was too rough," stammered Wat, "but then I always am a bear."

"A bear! Nay, it was to save my life."

"It was all past in a minute," said Alice.

"But thy hands. I hope mother has bound them up skilfully. Is the
pain great?"

"Prithee speak not of it again!" cried Wat in desperation.

It was curious, however, how content he was to remain in his present
position, which Hugh fancied must be terribly irksome to him, Wat
always finding it most difficult to sit still when anything active was
going on. It made him fear that he might be more hurt than they
knew. But the bonfires were in full blaze, and every great crackle and
leap of flame caused Thomasin to tremble, so that Wat's presence and
protection were very grateful to her. And to him it was a new
experience to be appealed to and looked up to as if he were a man; he
found it exceedingly pleasant, he had never believed it could be so
pleasant before. Mistress Tirell would have him go home with them,
having an ointment which she thought excellent for burns, and
though Thomasin could not endure to look upon the dressing, Wat
thought her interest and sympathy showed the kindest heart in the
world. In fact, it seemed to him that no one ever had been so sweet,

and when he got back late, he was very angry that Hugh should be too sleepy to listen to his outpourings of admiration.

As for Hal, he had to keep out of his way all day, Wat scarce being able to withhold his hands from him, while to Hugh he talked perpetually of what had happened, and put numberless questions as to what he thought about it all.

"She was a silly maiden," said Hugh, bluntly, "to shriek and run like a frightened hare."

"Much thou knowest!" cried the indignant Wat. "Thou wouldst have had her sit and be burned, forsooth!"

"Well, 'tis no matter of mine. Thou hast thy hands burned so thou canst not work, and had to sit up like the master himself—poor Wat! I was sorry for thee!"

"It was not so bad," said Wat, meditatively. "When thou art a grown man, thou wilt not care so much for all that foolish boy's play. I shall have no more of it."

Hugh burst into a laugh, as he shaped the graceful curve of a vine tendril.

"What has come to thee? Who was mad yesterday at having to play Master Sobersides?"

"I shall play the fool no more, I tell thee. What age, think you, might Mistress Thomasin be?"

"Nay, I scarce looked at her."

"I am going soon to the house to have my hands dressed."

"What need for that when the goodwife here could do it?"

"I could scarce be such a churl as to refuse when I was bidden," said Wat, hotly.

Hugh stared at him, not understanding the change from the Wat who fled the company of his elders, caring for none but hare-brained prentices; and as the days went by he grew more and more puzzled. Wat's hands seemed long in getting well, at any rate they required to be frequently inspected by Mistress Tirell, and it was remarkable that he could talk of naught but his new friends. He had always preferred the carving of curious and grotesque creatures, leaving all finer and more graceful work to Hugh. But now he implored Hugh to let him have the fashioning of a small kneeling angel.

"Thou!" cried the other, amazed. "What has put that into thy head? It is not the work that thou carest for."

"I have a mind for it when my hands are well. Prithee, Hugh!"

"Nay, thou wilt stick some grinning face on the poor angel's shoulders."

"Not I. I am going to try to shape something like Mistress Thomasin—well, why dost thou laugh?"

"What has come to thee, Wat? Since that day in the meadows it has been naught but Thomasin, Thomasin! Now I think of it, perhaps the fairies bewitched thee, since it was Midsummer Eve!" Perhaps Master Gervase guessed more clearly than Hugh what was the magic that had wrought this change, for though he laughed a good deal, he kept Wat occupied after the first three or four days were past, and Prothasy undertook to do all that was now necessary for the hurt hands. It was remarkable that under her care they seemed to improve more rapidly than at one time appeared probable, so that it was not very long before Wat was able to handle his chisel again, though from the great sighs he emitted Hugh was afraid the pain might be more than he allowed.

But now were no more pranks or junketings for Wat, no more liberties permitted from the prentices whose merry company he had hitherto preferred. He had suddenly awakened to a dignified sense of his position as journeyman, and Roger himself did not maintain it more gravely. Most remarkable, however, was the change in his appearance. It had always been an affront to Prothasy that Wat would never keep his clothes tidy or clean, she vowed he was a disgrace to their house, and that no others in the town made such a poor appearance. But now—now times indeed were changed! Now was Wat going off to the draper's to purchase fine cloth, and taking it himself to the Tailors' Guild, and most mighty particular was he about the cut of his sleeves. And as for his shoes, he ran to outrageous lengths in the toes—he who had always inveighed against the oafs who were not content with modest points! On the first Sunday on which Wat, thus attired, set forth, carrying a posy of lilies in his hand, and walking with such an air of conscious manliness as quite impressed those who met him, Hugh and Joan, with Agrippa, watching from the balcony, saw him turn up to St. Martin's Gate, and both burst out laughing.

"What has come to Wat?" cried Hugh. "Didst see his posy?"

"That is for Thomasin," Joan answered, nodding her pretty little head, "for I heard him ask mother what flowers maidens loved, and mother laughed, and said 'twas so long since she was a girl, she had forgotten, but if it was meant for Thomasin he had best ask Mistress Tirell. And I know Thomasin loves lilies. I wonder why Wat likes Thomasin so much? I like Alice better. But he is for ever talking about her yellow hair and her blue eyes, and wanting to hear if I have seen her pass. Look, Hugh, what a fierce-looking man!"

"That is he they call Henry of Doune, and Sir Adam Fortescue is stopping his horse to speak with him. And here comes Peter the shereman, and Nat the cordwainer. They say that. Earl Hugh has been quarrelling with the mayor again, and threatening to stop all the fishing in the Exe. Thy father is very wroth; he says the city bears it too tamely, and should complain to the king."

"Hugh, tell me about thy corbel. Hast thou thought it out?"

"I am always thinking. I see such beautiful lines and curves in my dreams that I am quite happy—till I wake."

"Father says in two or three months there will be a beginning, and I don't know what to wish," continued Joan. "I want both of you to do the best."

"There is no fear. I cannot match with the master."

"There is no other that can match with thee then!" cried Joan, fondling Agrippa. "He first and thou second—that is what it must be."

Hugh shook his head.

"Franklyn and Roger."

"They can work but they cannot design like thee," returned Joan, eagerly. "Roger will be mad to be the best, but—unless he steals a design—there is no chance of that. Oh, thou foolish Hugh, to make me tell thee this over and over again when thou knowest it better than I do!"

Chapter Thirteen.

By Proxy.

All through the autumn and early winter Hugh's thoughts were busy about the corbel work. He might have been impatient that it was not begun before, but that he knew the delay to have been gained for himself by Elyas, who had met with some opposition from certain canons of the Cathedral. They objected that it was unwise to put a work of such importance into the hands of a young apprentice. Every month gained, therefore, was in his favour, and the bishop remained his friend. The rough blocks were already in their places, ready for ordinary workmen to "boss them out," and by the end of February, which had been a wet and cheerless month, this was done.

Gervase was very much in the Cathedral superintending; Prothasy complained that she never saw him, and even Joan failed to coax him out. He was like a boy in his longing to begin, saying, and justly, that he was for ever over-seeing and correcting, and got little opportunity of letting his own powers have play. To Hugh, more freely than to any, he talked of his design, discussing its details with him; but one day Wat, looking uncomfortable, pulled Hugh after him as he went down the street.

"Talk a little less loudly with the master of what his *surs* is to be like," he said.

"Why?"

"Because there are those who would give their ears to have some notions in their thick brains, and would filch other folks' without scruple."

"Roger?"

"Ay, Roger is ever conveniently near when there is aught to be heard, and he is mad because the men say thy work is sure to be the best—after the master's. So beware, for the master thinks all as honourable as himself. What's this?"

For by this time they had got near the conduit and the market, and a crowd of people were coming along hooting and jeering some object, which, as they approached, turned out to be a man seated on a horse with his face to the tail, and a loaf hanging round his neck.

"Why, 'tis Edmund the baker!" cried Wat in great excitement. "Look how white he is—as white as his own meal! This comes of adulterating his bread, and now he will be put in the pillory, and his oven destroyed. Which wilt thou go to see, Hugh?"

"Neither. And what will Mistress Thomasin say of thy caring to see a man pilloried?"

"Oh, Mistress Thomasin, she is too dainty and fine! Her sister is more to my mind. Come!"

But Hugh would not. He left Wat, and walked down the High Street, and across the bridge with its houses and its chapel, and out into the country. A high wind was driving grey clouds swiftly across the sky, and now and then a dash of rain came in his face. The year was forward, and already buds were swelling, and the country showing the first signs of spring. Though so many years had passed Hugh could never walk in this direction without remembering his first coming to Exeter. How glad his father would be to know how it was with him! He was in the last year of his apprenticeship, and receiving wages of ten shillings a month, no small sum in those days. That he had got on in his craft and satisfied his master Hugh was aware, and now before him opened such an honourable task as a lad of his age could not have hoped for; what Stephen had longed for was about to come to pass, and Hugh knew that it was possible for him to bring fame and honour to his father's name.

With such thoughts, too, necessarily was joined very deep gratitude to Master Gervase. He had never faltered in his kindness; had Hugh been his own son he could not have trained him more carefully, or taught him more freely, with no grudging thoughts of possible rivalship. He had given the boy of his best, and Hugh's heart swelled as he recognised it, wondering whether it would ever be in his power to do something by way of return. Poor Hugh! He little thought how soon the occasion would come!

Then, as ever, he fell to studying the beautiful spring of branch and twig, and shaped and twisted them in his own mind, and saw them fair and perfect in the corbel, as artists see their works before they begin to carry them out, as yet unmarred by failure. Some of these models he bore home to study at leisure, and in the doorway met Elyas.

"I was looking for thee. John Hamlyn and I have had our commission to begin, and we are to hear about thee in two or three days. Have no fear. The bishop and I are strong enough to carry the matter; beshrew me, am I not the one to judge who is the best workman?"

"I may get the block ready for you, sir?" said Hugh eagerly.

"That may'st thou not, for I have already spoken to Ned Parsons, and he is there at this moment. Why, thou silly lad, disappointed? Thinkest thou that seeing thee set to do the rough labour will dispose them to choose thee for the better? Nay, nay, leave it to me, and do thou perfect thy design, remembering that it is a great and holy work to which thou art admitted. And hark ye, Hugh, spare no time in the design, and be not over-bold. Take something simple, such as ivy with the berries. Do that well, and it may be a second will fall to thy share."

No need to bid him be industrious. Hugh flung himself into it with such intensity of purpose that for the next day or two he could hardly eat or sleep. Wat, whose fate was also in the balance, took it with the utmost philosophy, said he should do his best, hoped that would turn out better than he expected, and snored peacefully the moment he was in his bed. Roger, who was certain to have the work, was as absorbed as Hugh, but silent withal. His nature was moody and suspicious, he gave no confidence, and Wat was not far wrong when he said that he was on the watch for what he could gather as to the designs of the others. Hugh generally drew his fancies on a bit of board with a stick sharpened and burnt. Usually he rubbed them out as soon as he had them to his fancy, but once or twice he had left them about, and was little aware how Roger had made them his own, or what exact copies were stowed away in a box.

THE CANON WATCHING HUGH AT WORK.   p. 223.

It was a week after Hugh's walk outside the walls that he saw Elyas come into the yard with Master William Pontington, the canon of St. Peter's, who a few years before had bought Poltimore of Lord Montacute. Hugh's heart beat so fast that his hand was scarcely so firm as usual, and he chipped the feather of a bird's wing. For something in Gervase's face told him that he brought news. Wat was working in the Cathedral. Presently the master and the canon came and stood behind Hugh. Hugh's hand trembled no more; he cut with astonishing freedom and power, feeling himself to be in a manner on his trial. Yet the silence seemed to him to last almost beyond endurance. He could not see the proud look on his master's face, nor watch the change of expression from cold indifference to eager interest on that of the canon. His own work never reached his hopes or his intentions, and he was far more quick to see its faults than its beauties. Suddenly he felt a hand on his shoulder.

"Enough, goodman," said a voice, "I give in. Since I have seen this young springald of thine at work, I own thou hadst a right to praise him as thou hast done. Give him a corbel and let him fall to at it as if it were this capital he is carving now, for the bird and her nest are as cunning a piece of workmanship as I have ever beheld."

"Thank his reverence, Hugh," said Gervase gleefully.

But Hugh turned red and then white, and could scarce stammer out the words.

"Ay, ay," said the canon good-humouredly, "no need for more; and I am glad thy heart is so set upon it, because now thy heart will go into thy hand, and, to tell thee the truth, that is what I feared might be wanting in such a young worker. Is that truly all thine own design?"

"The other men would be more like to come to Hugh than Hugh to go to them, holy sir," put in Elyas.

The canon, indeed, could scarcely believe his eyes. He made the young man show more of his carving, heard something of his father's skill, to all of which he had hitherto turned a deaf ear, and departed, ready to do battle for Hugh against any who spoke a disparaging word.

"There goes thy most persistent opponent," said Elyas, coming back and rubbing his hands in glee; "'twas all I could do to bring him here, and he grumbled the whole way about putting work into inexperienced hands, and I know not what! Now to-morrow, Hugh, Ned Parsons will have finished his blocking out for me, and I will set him to thine. I shall give thee the first pillar in the choir on the opposite side to mine own. It is not so well in view as some of the others, but that should make no difference in its fairness. And here is Joan to be told the news."

Joan shook her wise little head over it, and opined that now Hugh would be worse than ever in neither eating nor sleeping. But it was not so. He was very quiet all that day, and when work was over he and Joan set off for the Cathedral that he might look upon his pillar—with what longing eyes!—and picture it again and again to himself as it should be.

"And there is father's—shaped," said Joan; "how long and slender it looks! I do hope that his will be the most beautiful of all, because he is older, and because you have all learnt from him, and because—he is father and there is no one like him!"

"No fear!" said Hugh. "I have seen his designs. Not one of us can overpass him."

"Mother is not easy about him, either," said Joan, who had sat down and clasped her hands round her knees. "He has pains in his head and dizziness, and he will not have the leech because he says he talks so foolishly about Mars and Venus, and father says he does not believe the planets have aught to do with us. Dost thou think they have?"

"I know not," said Hugh unheeding. "Joan, hast thou heard where Roger's is to be?"

"On the same side with father's, and Wat opposite, and Franklyn between thee and Wat. Tell me once again how thine ivy is to curl."

From one cause or another there was a slight delay in the preparation of Hugh's block. Something hindered Ned Parsons, or he was slower in his work, or kept Mid-Lent too jovially; at any rate there was a check which seemed very terrible to Hugh, and Roger and Wat were both at work before him. Wat intended to carry out a bold design of leaf and fruit, but he vowed that something grotesque there must be, and if he might not put Agrippa there, he should have a neighbour's dog which had shown a great liking for him. It must be owned that Wat was of a somewhat fickle disposition, his fancy for angels and lily-bearing maidens was over, and Mistress Thomasin was betrothed to a rich burgess. It seemed likely that he would lose his heart and find it again many a time before the final losing took place.

Meanwhile it was evident to more than the wife that something was amiss with Elyas. He was at work on his corbel, but heavy-headed and depressed, finding the carving for which he had longed a labour, and not really making good progress. Of this he was fully conscious, so conscious indeed, that a fear evidently oppressed him that his hand might have lost its power, and he spoke of it anxiously to Hugh.

"I wot not why it is," he said, wearily passing his hand across his face, "but though I know what I have to do, I fail in the doing. Come with me to-day, Hugh, and see for thyself."

And, indeed, Hugh, when he had mounted the ladder and raised the cloth concealing the carving, was fain to acknowledge that it was as Gervase said. Instead of the firm and powerful strokes which marked his work in all stages, there was a manifest feebleness, hesitation, and blurring which filled Hugh with dismay. It was only the beginning; nothing was there which might not be set right, but what if indeed his skill was failing? He could hardly bear to meet the questioning in Gervase's eyes.

"Master—it—it—"

"Speak out—speak freely," said Elyas hoarsely. "It is bad work?"

"It is not as thy work. Thou art ill, and thy hand feeble; wait a little, and let the sickness pass."

The other shook his head.

"Nay, I dread to wait. Something, some fear of the morrow drives me on. Hugh, this on which I have set my heart—is it to be snatched from me? I see it before me, fair and beautiful, a joy for generations to come. I can do it. I have never failed before, how can I fail now? And yet, and yet—"

He covered his face with his hands. Hugh, inexpressibly moved, laid his hand on his arm.

"Sir, dear sir, it is only a passing malady. In a few days you will look back and smile at your fears. Come home and let Mistress Prothasy make you a cooling drink."

But Elyas was obstinately determined to work while he could. Haunted by a fear of disabling sickness, unable to believe that the next stroke he made would not show all his old vigour, he toiled, struggled, and went home more disheartened than ever. Yet there were no absolute marks of illness about him, and Prothasy was neither fanciful nor over-anxious, and the next day thought him better. Work over, Hugh went up to his room to perfect his designs, for presently he was to begin. With his board and burnt stick he traced in full the ivy clusters upon which he had decided, carrying out all the smallest details, so that he might have it well in his mind before he put his tool to the stone.

Satisfied he was not, but yet it seemed to him that the lines were fairly good, and it was broad and simple, such as Gervase had suggested. He had finished and was holding it at arm's length to search for shortcomings when he was startled by a cry, and the next moment heard Joan's voice calling wildly, "Hugh, Hugh!"

Hugh dashed the board on the ground, and rushed towards the cry. He found Prothasy kneeling on the ground, holding her husband's head in her lap, while Joan, with a terror-struck face, was unfastening his vest as well as her trembling little hands would allow.

"The leech!" was all Prothasy could say, and Hugh was out of the door the same moment, flying down the street in pursuit of the first apothecary he could find, so that they were back before Prothasy had dared to hope. It appeared that Elyas had but just come in from the Cathedral, when, without warning, he dropped on the ground, cutting his head against a sharp projection. He remained unconscious for many hours, and the leech looked grave, the more so when it was found that all one side was affected, so that his arm and leg were useless.

A heavy sadness hung over the house, even Hal hushing his malapert tongue. The warden was greatly beloved by all; they were, moreover, extremely proud of his genius, and now—was that strong right hand to lie helpless! As the news spread some of the families near sent their serfs to ask tidings; the good bishop came himself, full of grief.

"Truly, goodwife," he said to Prothasy, "this blow falls heavy on us all. I know not what we can do without him, he has been the very spring of our work, ever cheerful, ever ready, seeing to everything; in good sooth we have had in him a support on which we have leaned more heavily than we knew."

Prothasy stood up, white and cold, and apparently unmoved. Very few were aware of the tempest which raged in her heart; bitter remorse for many sharp words, passionate love, sickening anxiety. She had often been jealous of the work which seemed to absorb Elyas, and many a time had flouted him for some kind action of which she was secretly proud, and against which she would not have said a word had she not known well that he would not be shaken from it. And the worst was, that so strong had grown the habit, that she was conscious now, in the midst of what was little short of torture, that were he to recover from his sickness it would be the same thing again. Joan little knew with what a weary longing her mother looked at her—to be a child again, to have no chain of habit binding her round and round, to be free!

For a few days the works in the Cathedral were stopped. The bishop ordered this as a mark of respect to Gervase, the most self-denying mark he could pay. There were many things to carry out in the yard, and Franklyn, looking wretched, and perhaps, like Prothasy, bearing a burden of self-reproach, kept strict rule, and would permit no idling. Hugh, however, could be little there. After Gervase recovered his consciousness it was plain enough that he liked Hugh to be with him.

They sometimes thought, from the wistful look in his eyes, that he wanted to say something, but as yet his speech was unintelligible. Wat was of no use in the sick-room; it was always impossible for him not to make more noise than two or three others put together, even when he was walking on tip-toe, and painfully holding his breath. But in the house he was invaluable, thought nothing a trouble, would run here and there, fetch the apothecary or the leech, or walk miles on any errands they could devise. When three or four days had passed, and hope had strengthened, Hugh found him one day belabouring Hal Crocker for having ventured to tease Agrippa. Hal took advantage of the newcomer to wriggle himself off and escape, making a face at Wat as he did so.

"That is the most incorrigible varlet in the town," said Wat, looking after him wrathfully. "Now, is aught wanted?"

"No. He is sleeping."

"He will soon be himself again," said the other, joyfully, "and thou wilt set to work."

They were both young and both hopeful.

"Ay, so I think," returned Hugh. "And thou, too?"

"Mine will not do the master much credit, though I have got a fancy for my dog. When we are all gone and forgotten, there will Spot be, gazing down on a fresh generation of citizens. Think of that, Hugh! What will they be like, I wonder? New faces and new fashions. Come up the street with me. The itinerant justices came this morning, and I want to know what they have done to the forestaller whom they caught half-way to Brampford Speke, meeting the people on their way to market Roger said he was to have two years in gaol."

"Wat?"

"Ay."

"I wanted to ask thee. Thou rememberest the day the master was taken?"

"Ay."

"I was in our room, and had just drawn out my design on the board."

"Ay, thy head was full of thy old *surs*. Well?"

"When I heard them cry I ran down and flung it on the ground, and it is gone."

"Gone! Oh, that thief Roger!"

"Thou thinkest so?"

"Thinkest? Who else? It was not I—nor Agrippa. Hast thou asked?"

"Ay, and he was very wroth."

Wat doubled his fists and made several significant movements.

"That is what he has been trying for—to get at thy designs, thine or the master's. How couldst thou be such an oaf?"

"Who could think of it then?"

"He could, at any rate. He would think how to push himself to the front if he had to do it over all our dead bodies. Say good-bye to thy design, friend Hugh!"

"Nay, I'll not bear it," cried the young man, angrily; "if he use my design I'll proclaim it through the town. And he works fast, and will get the advantage of me, because the master will not spare me while he is so ill. Out on him, what can I do?"

"Change thy design," advised Wat, sagely. "To whom canst thou complain with the goodman ill? Franklyn ever favours Roger."

There was truth enough in the words to make Hugh very angry with the feeling of having been treacherously dealt with, and of having no means of righting himself. When, the next day, Roger went off to the Cathedral, rightly or wrongly Wat and Hugh fancied there was an air of triumph about him, which was infuriating. Hugh could not be spared, but Wat vowed he would make out by one means or another what he was intending to carve. He began by coming up to him as he stood at the foot of the ladder choosing his chisel, and asking what was his subject. It took Wat rather aback when Roger stared full in his face and answered, "Ivy."

"Ivy! What, the same as Hugh?"

"I know naught of Hugh."

"That thou didst then. Thou hast heard him speak of it a dozen times."

"I have better things to do than to listen to idle prentice talk."

"The master can witness that thou heardest."

"Let him—when he can!" said Roger, with a hard laugh.

"Now, out on thee for a false loon!" cried Wat.

He might have said more but that two of the chapter were close at hand, and he flung himself away with a heart full of rage, and betook himself to his own corbel, on which he vented a good deal of force which he would gladly have employed in pommelling Roger. And this having a calming effect, he came to the conclusion that it would be best for Hugh to take no notice of the older man's perfidy. There was no proof that Roger had stolen the design, there was nothing except honour to prevent his using the same foliage, and with Gervase ill, an accusation might meet with little attention, and perhaps harm Hugh more than Roger.

Wat groaned, and dug in his tool with a violence which it cost him no little trouble to repair.

Perhaps Hugh was helped to patience by the circumstances of Gervase's illness. There was something so infinitely sad in this sudden check at the time when all the master's hopes seemed to be on the point of touching fulfilment, that such a disappointment as Hugh's must be comparatively trifling. He was young, he could wait. Besides, he would not count it as a disappointment, it was only a delay. Elyas was already better, and probably in another week he would be free. And meanwhile, if his design had been filched, he would work out another—that he could do while in Gervase's room, and his hopes rose high. He had chosen the ivy because the master had counselled simple forms, but he felt as if now, with this taken from him, he was free to try a higher flight, and he fell hopefully to work with all the glad consciousness of power.

Elyas was better, but his speech remained much affected, and as his strength returned, there were an evident restlessness and anxiety which were alarming. It became, indeed, clear that something weighed on his mind, and the leech showed more common sense than was usual with him when he pronounced that, unless the trouble could be removed, it might go hardly with his patient. Everybody, frightened out of their wits by this prediction, tried their best to find out what was amiss. Prothasy tried—with a patience which no one had seen in her before. Joan tried—laying her pretty head fondly upon the poor useless right hand. Hugh tried—and sometimes they fancied that his efforts came nearest to the hidden trouble, though never quite reaching it. Hugh spoke of the Cathedral works, of how Franklyn, Roger, Wat, and two other men had begun, of how glad all would be when Elyas himself was able to be there again. And then, fancying that perhaps he feared lest another should touch his corbel, he told him that the bishop himself had said it should wait for him even were all the others finished.

A feeble—so feeble as to be almost imperceptible—shake of the head made Hugh impress this the more strongly, and then followed a painful effort to make them understand something, of which they could not gather the right meaning. It was terrible to Prothasy—almost more, indeed, than she could bear.

The bishop heard of this drawback, for the warden's anxiety and distress had the worst effect upon his strength, and they began very much to fear that if they were not removed they might lead to another attack more serious than the last. He came himself to see Gervase with the hope of fathoming the trouble; and at any rate his visit gave pleasure, for the sick man's eyes brightened as the bishop stood in the doorway and uttered the words of peace. They could even make out a murmur of "This is kind."

Bishop Bitton sat on the stool which Prothasy put for him, and set himself to chat about all that was going on in the Cathedral. Then he said—

"We think there is something on thy mind, goodman, which thou canst not explain, and which retards thy recovery. It may be that I can arrive at it, but do not try to speak. Here lies thy left hand. When thou wouldst say Ay, lift thy forefinger so, and for Nay, keep thy hand still. Now, first, is there something thou wouldst say?"

The finger was raised.

The good bishop nodded, proud of his ingenuity.

"Hath it aught to do with thy spiritual condition?"

No sign.

"Or thy worldly matters? Nay. Thy wife? Thy child? Any of thy relations? Nay, to all. Then we will come to municipal matters. Doth anything there weigh on thee? Still nay. Thy guild?"

The bishop persisted in a string of questions which brought no response, before arriving at the subject of the Cathedral, which in his own mind he doubted not was where the trouble lay. Indeed, his first question as to whether it were not so, brought the lifted finger, and a hopeful gleam in the eyes. Only Prothasy was in the room, Hugh having gone down to the yard.

But, try as he might, the bishop found his task very difficult. They narrowed the matter at last to the corbel, but Elyas got restless and irritable with making efforts to speak and explain himself, and the bishop laid his hand finally upon his arm, saying kindly—

"Have patience. We shall reach it in time. Thou dost but fever thyself with vain struggles. Hearken. I have assured thee that we will wait months, ay, years if thou wilt, till God gives back thy strength. Is that what thou desirest?"

No sign.

"Nay?" repeated the bishop, in some surprise. He paused, and then bent forward. "Wouldst thou then have another take the work? Ay? And carry out thy designs? Ay, again. Goodman, were that not a pity? A little patience and thy strength may come back, the leech says—"

But his words died away before the look which the sick man turned on him. He looked away to collect himself.

"If it must be so," he said at length, hesitatingly. "Goodwife, you understand it as I do? It is no doing of ours."

"Nay, my lord, it is clearly his wish," said Prothasy firmly.

"And now," Bishop Bitton continued, "we must know to whom thou wouldst confide it. The other warden, John Hamlyn, ranks next to thee." But it was evident that Gervase would have none of John Hamlyn.

"Walter Bennet?"

No.

"Well, it is natural thou wouldst keep it in thine own yard. William Franklyn, thy head man?"

Still no.

The bishop pondered; named two other skilled workmen, and received no assent.

"Thou thinkest well of thy Roger? Nay, again!—Wat?—who remains, goodman? Thy prentice Hugh is too young."

But to the good bishop's amazement Elyas, looking eagerly at him, raised, not the finger only, but the whole hand.

"Hugh! Thou wouldst choose Hugh! Bethink thee that he is but a prentice, and when we gave him the work it was thought that thou wouldst advise and help him."

Still there could be no doubt that this was the master's desire; Hugh and none but Hugh was to carry out his design, and carve his corbel. The bishop shook his head doubtfully, but he could not gainsay Elyas;

there was so much relief apparent in his face, and his lips moved as if in thankfulness.

"It shall be as thou wilt," he said gravely.

He told Prothasy that she must use her judgment and send Hugh to his work when Elyas could spare him, and went away, doubtful, it must be owned, of his own wisdom in handing over one of the most prominent of the corbels to the youngest of the carvers.

Chapter Fourteen.

Will Roger Succeed?

Hugh's first feeling was one of bitter and intense disappointment. He cared not one jot about the position of the corbel, what he did care for was the working out his own design, seeing that, as it were, spring into life under his hand. It was a very different thing to carry out another man's, for, however good the execution might be, that could not equal the joy of creation. He turned quite white when Prothasy told him, thinking the news should give him proud delight, but, curiously enough, Joan, who was in the room, child as she was, understood his feelings better, and the moment her mother left slipped her hand in his.

"Alack, alack, poor Hugh!"

"There go all my hopes," he groaned.

"But it is for father," she urged. "Bethink you how grievous it is for him to have no hand in what he longed for."

"I think of my father, too. I wanted to credit his name."

"Nay," said Joan softly, "if he could speak he would say there were nobler things than fame."

Was not that really what he had said, and was it not strange that she should repeat it? But then Joan ever had strange thoughts for her age, and Hugh's better nature came to his aid.

"In good sooth, thou art right, Joan," he said after a pause. "Whatever it cost me, I will remember that I might not be working in the Cathedral at all were it not for the master. I will put aside thought of my own fancies, and carry his out with my might."

There was something solemn about this promise, and both felt it so, Joan looking up admiringly into Hugh's face, and more certain than ever that—her father always excepted—there was no one like him in the world.

Gervase gave better signs of mending after the bishop's visit, and his speech began slowly to clear itself, but they soon found that he was anxious for Hugh to begin work, and that the latter might now leave him to the care of Prothasy and Joan. He made Hugh bring his design to his side, and evidently wished him to go through it there and to show that he fully understood it. It was a conventional design, mixed with foliage, long, slender, and sharply cut, not unlike the lower leaves of the shepherd's purse greatly magnified, and depending for its beauty upon certain strongly marked curves. It had never seemed to Hugh quite equal to the master's other designs.

There was much wonder and some jealousy of Hugh when Gervase's choice became known; but also general satisfaction, there being much competition in the matter, and no one being willing to give up his own chance of distinguishing himself by producing and carrying out a design which should surpass all the others. No one, that is to say, but Wat. He had the lowest opinion of his own powers, and thought it sheer folly to have been chosen for such a task, and he would very gladly have made over his pillar to Hugh, and faithfully carried out the master's drawings. As, however, this was impossible, he set himself to perpetuate Spot, and at the same time to keep a watchful eye upon Roger.

Roger was the best pleased of all, for, since Hugh could no longer use his own design, it was pretty sure that no one would interfere with him. He was a first-rate workman, only wanting in imagination and invention; he had no fear but that now he had provided himself with the design, his corbel would hold its own with, perhaps surpass, all others. He even managed to smooth certain ruffles in his conscience by assuring it that since Hugh could not have undertaken any independent labour, no harm was done to him; ivy had always been in his mind, and he had but assisted his fancy by a means which had fallen in his way.

Nevertheless, it was remarkable that he took the utmost pains to prevent Wat from getting a sight of his work. The carvings were always covered when left for the night, and there was a sort of tacit understanding that no one need openly display his work, although often one called another to give advice upon some doubtful point. But Roger used unusual precautions to arrange his materials and himself as he worked, so as completely to hide the carving from view. Wat pondered long upon this, and at last, coming home with Hugh one evening, he asked—

"The design which Roger filched, is it yet in thy head?"

"Ay," briefly answered Hugh.

"Draw it out then again."

"Where is the use? I shall never have the chance of using it, and if I had, I could not now when that false loon has had all this time to push on with his."

"Still—do as I bid thee," returned Wat obstinately.

Nor would he rest until he had the design safely in his keeping. Then he carried it to Prothasy.

"Prithee, goodwife, hast thou any place where thou canst bestow this safely?"

"What for?"

"It is Hugh's design for the corbel which he was to have carved: one he did before, and has never seen since the day the master was taken ill."

"There are places in the yard without lumbering the house."

"Ay, mistress, but I would have thee keep it where none of us, not even Hugh himself, should ever see it. He hath marked the day of the month upon it—see."

She looked questioningly at him, then took the board without a word, and carried it away with her, while Wat rubbed his hands and pushed back the lathes of the window to whistle to Spot, who, as usual, was basking lazily in the sun on the opposite side of the street.

Hugh worked with all his might. His chief difficulty consisted in the extreme anxiety of bishop and chapter, who were really terror-struck at the idea of so young a workman having so great a responsibility thrust upon him, particularly without the master being there to oversee. Constantly one or another was coming, desiring to speak with him, and urging him if he were in any doubt to seek counsel from the older men. When he answered modestly enough that he would do so if he felt he needed help, but that at present he found no difficulty, they looked the more anxious and uncomfortable, shook their heads, and said it was impossible that he could have the necessary experience. All this was sufficiently depressing, but Hugh found comfort in Gervase's evident faith in him. He was so far recovered that his speech had come back, and a certain amount of power in the disabled arm; he could get about the house and even listen to Franklyn's account of the work done; but his supreme pleasure lay in hearing Hugh's report of his work at what Elyas ever called *his* corbel, and his chief longing was for the time when he should get down and see it with his own eyes, though that day they feared was far away.

He laughed over Hugh's description of the fears of the canons, and managed to see the bishop and to assure him so confidently of his prentice's power to carry through the task entrusted to him, that Bishop Bitton, who had hitherto doubted whether it had not been the fancy of a sick man, was completely reassured, and tried Hugh no more with advice to seek counsel. The chaunter or precentor, however, was not to be persuaded. He was a sour little man, who liked to be in opposition, and one day came bustling up to the foot of the ladder on which Hugh was at work, intimating that he wished to speak to him. Hugh accordingly came down, though not with the best grace in the world, for he knew very well what he was likely to hear.

"Young lad," said the precentor, pursing his mouth and throwing out his chest, "it appears to me that this task is beyond thy years."

Hugh was silent, standing gazing down at the precentor. His face was much the same as it had been when he was a child, fair and ruddy, with light hair and honest grey eyes, which looked full in the face of those who talked with him. He was tall and very powerfully made; with promise indeed, in a few years' time, of unusual strength and size.

"As it has been rashly, over-rashly to my thinking, committed to thee, I say nothing," the precentor continued; "we must bear the risk. But that should not prevent precaution. I desire, therefore, that thou wilt call upon the older men to counsel thee, and correct thy mistakes. From what I learn, thou hast done naught of this; thou art too self-satisfied, too presumptuous, and we, forsooth, must suffer for thine overweening confidence. See that thou act as I desire."

Hugh did not immediately answer, perhaps finding some difficulty in keeping back hasty words. When he did speak it was to ask a question.

"Reverend sir," he said, "who of all our guild would know best what I can or cannot do?"

The precentor hesitated.

"Thy master—in health," he added, with emphasis on the last word.

"Before aught ailed him, he was set upon my carving a corbel."

"Ay, but not a forward one, such as this, and not without his being here to overlook thee. This is another matter."

"It may be so, reverend sir. In good sooth, I found it hard to give up my own work and take his, but since it pleasured him, and since he can trust it in my hands, I must work, if I work at all, without such let or hindrance as you would put on me. You say truly that it is a great task. I cannot carry it out fettered and cramped. If the Lord Bishop and his chapter hold that I have forfeited the trust they committed to me, I would humbly pray to be allowed to resign it. If it is left in my hands, then I must be as the other men, free to work undisturbed."

Hugh spoke with great modesty, yet so firmly as to amaze the little precentor, who had thought he might meet with a boy's petulance, which he was determined to put down. He would have liked to take Hugh at his word and dismiss him, but this he could not venture to do, since the bishop, though he had had his fears, thought highly of the lad's genius, and would have strongly resented any such high-handed act. He found himself in a position for which he was quite unprepared, obliged to withdraw his commands, but he was not the man to do this frankly or fully.

"Thou art a malapert springald to bandy words with me," he said angrily. "Thou, a mere prentice, to put thyself on a level with other men! This comes of being cockered and made much of, out of thy fit place. But I shall speak with the bishop, and I wot we shall see whether thine insolence is to go unchastised."

He spoke loud enough for some of the other men to hear, and marched off, leaving Hugh very angry, though he had been able to control all outward signs of wrath. He went up his ladder again, hearing a chuckle of laughter among the others, and feeling sore and bitter with all the world.

"As if it were not enough to have given up what I had thought of so long," he muttered, looking round at the corbel on the other side, which, somewhat to his surprise, no one had yet been set upon, "but I must be flouted at for failing when I have scarce begun, and set to ask counsel from—whom? Roger, maybe, Roger, who could not do his own task without stealing from my wits! Well, I have finely angered the precentor, and it will be no wonder if it is all stopped, and I am sent off, though I said naught that was unbecoming, or that I should not be forced to say again. I will tell the master, and he shall judge."

The precentor was indeed very angry, and the first person he met, and to whom he poured out his indignation, was Master William Pontington, the canon, who had been one of the last to admit the possibility of the prentice being allowed to undertake the carving of a corbel.

"This," said the precentor solemnly, "this comes of the bishop's weak—hem—over-easiness. If he permitted such a thing, it should have been under control and direction, instead whereof we have a young jackanapes perched up there, and left to amuse himself as he likes, and telling me—telling me to my very face—that he is as good as any other!"

It was well-known among the chapter that the precentor never omitted a chance of saying a word against the bishop, and the canon smiled.

"The dean thinks as well of the lad as doth the bishop," he said. "My counsel is to leave him alone. If he be trusted with a man's work, we must trust him as to the manner in which he carries it out, and not fret him with constant restrictions. Beshrew me, but were I in his place I should feel the same!"

So supported, Hugh was left very fairly at peace to toil at his carving, although even his friends among the chapter felt deep anxiety for the result, and tried hard to get peeps at what he had already done. But Hugh, having once suffered, was almost as careful as Roger to keep his work concealed, and as for Wat, he made a complete watch-dog of himself, staying the last of the workmen, and being one of the earliest to arrive. He cared far more for Hugh's success than for his own, and he was the only one who had seen the corbel. Somehow or other, however, perhaps from words he let drop, perhaps from glimpses caught of its progress, the report went about that it was very beautiful.

Every day Gervase eagerly questioned Hugh as to what progress he had made. Once or twice Hugh told him of changes he had made in the design—told him with some doubt lest it should displease him that his apprentice should dream of bettering his work. But Gervase was of a rarely generous nature, frankly acknowledging the improvement.

"I would I could get to see it; thou art right, thou art right, Hugh, that change takes off a certain stiffness. Do what thou wilt, I trust thee ungrudgingly, in spite of precentor or any of them. And they will have to own that we are in the right when they see it finished. Now, art ready for our game at chess?"

Slowly, but surely, the doubts and anxieties as to the lad's work died away, and instead of them grew up an impression that when the day came for its uncovering, something of great merit would be displayed. The one most affected by all these rumours was Roger. His own was progressing well, and he was the more eager not to be outdone; moreover, he had injured Hugh, and this very fact made his jealousy and dislike more bitter. If, after all, Hugh should surpass him! Roger gnawed his lip, and meditated day and night upon some possible means of preventing such a catastrophe. He would have given a great deal to see the carving and judge for himself, and he made several attempts in this direction, always baffled by Wat's vigilance. One day he got hold of Franklyn, and asked him what he heard of Hugh and his work. Franklyn was a narrow-minded man, but honest, and he answered openly, that from a glimpse he had caught, and from what the master had repeated, he doubted whether the lad had ever done anything so good before.

"He hath great power," added Franklyn musingly.

"Ay, to work at another man's design!" said Roger, with a sneer. "I call that another matter from working one's own."

"Marry amen! and so do I," said a voice, emphatically.

Roger started as if he had been stung. He had not known that Wat was just behind, and he knew too well the meaning of the words. But it made him the more bitter against Hugh.

Through those summer days work went on briskly in the Cathedral. All were fired with enthusiasm, partly from the bishop's example, partly from personal longing to distinguish themselves. The choir with its noble vaulting was completed, a splendid monument of Bitton's episcopate; but the corbels would be a prominent and beautiful feature in the work, and perhaps, with some prevision that his life would not be long, the bishop desired very greatly to see them finished. Hugh worked incessantly; he hoped before the summer was over to have brought his carving to an end. Gervase had been out several times, indeed his recovery was amazing, but now that matters had gone so far, he said that he should keep away from the Cathedral until Hugh's corbel was a finished work.

Hugh had been so much absorbed that he had thought little of Roger, although he did not relax any of his precautions as to keeping his work hidden, and Wat and Joan were far more watchful guardians than he dreamt of.

He had a great surprise one Sunday when they came in from St. Mary Arches, and he saw a big man standing in the doorway, which was still wreathed with the midsummer greenery, and looked at him at first as if he were a stranger. The man, in his turn, stared from one to the other as if in search of someone; something struck Hugh as familiar, and the next moment he sprang to his side and seized his hand.

"Master Andrew!" he cried in delight, "where have you come from? How long have you been here? Are you well? How is Moll?"

The sailor put his hands on his shoulders, held him at arm's length, and looked him up and down in amazement, which soon broadened into a laugh.

"I never thought to have found thee grown to this size!" he said; "thou art a man, and a proper one! Where have I come from? From Exmouth, and I would have sailed up in the *Queen Maud* if your burgesses of Exeter had not been fools enough to let a woman ruin their river for them with her weir. I have had a wish many a time to know how thou fared, and Friar Luke—we are good friends, what thinkest thou of that? I never thought to be friends with a grey friar— gives me no peace because I bring him no tidings. Thy father? Ay, anyone could see it was that way with him, honest man! And Agrippa?"

There was much to hear and tell. The warden took a great fancy to Andrew and would not listen to his going to a hostelry for the night, and Prothasy was pleased to see her husband interested. But the one who took most to Andrew, and who in his turn was greatly liked by the sailor, was Wat. Andrew vowed that Wat should have been a sailor, and Wat was almost ready to renounce everything in favour of the sea. Wat told him all about Hugh, and his work and his genius, and what great things were entrusted to him at the Cathedral, and promised to take there the next morning as early as the doors were opened, and Joan, Hugh, and Wat must all go forth after the five o'clock supper, and show him the castle and St. Nicolas' Priory, which he looked at with disfavour in spite of his friendship with Friar Luke, and the alms-houses of Saint Alexius, which pleased him better. All these, but more especially the bridge, made him own that Exeter was a very noble city.

Hugh could not go to the Cathedral as early as the others the next morning, because the master wanted some measurements taken, but he was to follow almost immediately, and there could not have been a prouder showman than Wat. He scarcely let Andrew glance round at the fair beauty of the building before he was off to fetch Hugh's ladder and to set it up against the pillar. They were, as he intended to be, the first there, and the covering might be safely taken off, but he was so prudent that he darted off to watch, calling to Andrew to go up and unwrap the covering for himself. As he stood in the nave, it struck him that he heard a cry, but he set it down to someone outside, and when some minutes had passed, and he thought time enough had been given, he hurried back, expecting to find the sailor full of admiration. Instead of this he met him coming towards him, looking, as even Wat could not fail to see, rather strangely disturbed. He said at once and roughly—

"Fine traps you set for strangers!"

"How, master?"

"How? In placing a ladder which has been cut through. Nay, I like not such jests."

"Cut through!" cried Wat, with such genuine amazement that Andrew looked keenly at him.

"Beshrew me, yes! Didst thou not know it? The ladder gave way, and I might have made a fool of myself on the stones below, but that I have been long enough on shipboard to hold on by the very hair of my head. I gave thee a halloo."

"I never thought it was thou, sir. Cut through! Then that is Roger's work again; he would have done Hugh a mischief, the false traitor! If only I could wring his neck! Let me see the place."

He strode off, boiling over with excitement, and Andrew, with a whistle of some amusement, sauntered slowly after him.

It was quite true. One of the rungs of the ladder about half-way up had been so cut where it ran into the upright that it must necessarily have given way under an ordinary weight, and Hugh, who would have gone up encumbered with his tools, could scarcely have avoided a bad fall. He arrived very soon, and the other men dropped in, Wat questioning them all closely, not, it must be owned, with any thought that they could have done such a dastardly deed, but with a hope of getting evidence that Roger had been seen near the ladder. In this he failed. No one had noticed anything, all the ladders lay near each other, and whoever had done it had undoubtedly exercised much caution and ingenuity. The men were angry. Many of them were jealous of Hugh, but not to the extent of committing a crime in order to incapacitate him; such an act, if proved, would be visited by the most severe punishment the guild could inflict. Roger himself came late, he cast a swift glance at the groups of men standing about in unusual idleness, and another, which Wat noted, towards Hugh's pillar. When he saw Hugh there, engaged on his work as on every other day, the colour left his face, and he glanced uneasily from one to the other, finally pausing before Wat, who had planted himself aggressively in his way.

"Is aught the matter?" he demanded.

"Murder or maiming might have been the matter," returned Wat grimly. "Now, maybe, there will be naught but the hanging."

"Hanging?"

"Of the villain who tried this wickedness. Canst thou give a guess who that might be?"

"Thou talkest riddles," said Roger impatiently. "Let me pass to my work."

"Ay," returned Wat, "pass. We others mean to find out who it is among us who filches designs, and cuts through ladders, and brings shame on all our body."

Flinging a glance of rage at him, Roger pushed by, and Wat went off to meet the other warden, John Hamlyn, and to lay the complaint before him. Andrew's presence and what he had himself experienced in the matter helped to make it serious, and the crime was sufficiently grave for the warden to promise that there should be a guild meeting to consider it.

"What evidence hast thou against Roger?"

"He hath done Hugh other harm, sir," answered Wat after a pause. "He hath stolen his designs."

"Take care, take care," said the warden warningly, "these be grave charges. How knowest thou? Hast thou seen his work?"

"Nay, sir. Nevertheless I can prove it, if you will."

"How then?"

"When the master was taken ill, Hugh's designs were stolen, but I made Hugh draw them out again, and Mistress Prothasy hath them in her keeping."

"But thou knowest not that there there thou hast what Roger is working upon. Tush, man, these are but idle tales. Thou must bring better proofs."

Wat was far more grave and sober than usual.

"I wot not if we shall get proofs of this last villainy," he said. "Someone hath done it, and no other bears Hugh a grudge. But the other, thou, sir, may'st prove for thyself if thou wilt."

"Prithee, how?"

"Come with me, sir, and get the board with the design from the goodwife. Thou wilt see by the date—Saint George's Day—that the carving was not far enough advanced for Hugh to have drawn his from that. Keep it by thee, Master Hamlyn, and when Roger's work is uncovered, judge for thyself."

"Thou hast not seen the corbel, thou sayest, and this is no more than thy fancy."

"No more. Yet I will stake my fair fame upon it," said Wat, boldly.

The warden hesitated, finally said the test was a fair one, and promised to come that evening and receive the board from Prothasy. This little arrangement partly compensated Wat for the failure to bring home any evidence connecting Roger with the ladder. At the same time a feeling had risen up against him among the other workmen, who felt that they were in a measure compromised until the offender was discovered, and Roger found himself treated to cold and doubtful looks, while even Franklyn appeared to have his confidence shaken. Hugh was the one who made least of the affair; he was so persuaded of Roger's ill-will that this fresh proof scarcely affected him, and it was he who induced Andrew—though more, it must be owned, for the credit of the guild than from any charitable feelings—to give up his plan of taking summary vengeance by administering a sound thrashing.

They were all sorry when Andrew departed, carrying not only messages for Moll and Friar Luke, but a scroll for this latter, written in Hugh's fairest penmanship, and a marvel to the whole household.

Chapter Fifteen.

"Here's a Coil!"

"Hugh, when will it be finished—truly? I am so weary of to-morrow, and to-morrow, and to-morrow, and it never gets any nearer! Father is longing, too, for all he pretends to be patient."

"It is finished now," answered Hugh, gloomily, "only I cannot keep my hands from it."

"In good sooth! And art not glad?"

"Nay. It is not what I would have it. I had such brave ideas, and they have all come to naught, as ever. Joan, will one ever be satisfied?"

"I have heard father say something about 'a noble discontent.' I did not understand it, but maybe this was in his mind. And I don't think he is ever satisfied with his own work. But thine is sure to be beautiful," cried Joan, brightening. "Is it really then to be to-morrow?"

"Nay; the bishop has decided that as four or five are nearly ready, they shall wait to be uncovered together on Lammas Day. The best is to have the choice of the other corbels."

"And which shalt thou choose?" demanded Joan securely.

"There will be no choosing for me. Master Hamlyn has a beautiful design of pears and apples, they say, and Franklyn of vine leaves, and there is that traitor Roger, he can work. I shall grudge it to him, but not to old Wat. Joan, I verily believe that Wat's will be one of the best."

"Hath he really stuck Spot up there?"

"Hath he not?" said Hugh, with a laugh. "There he is, to the life, at the base, but 'tis so cleverly done, and he thinks so little of it!"

"Lammas Day!" sighed Joan, "a whole three weeks! I shall get one of your tally sticks, and cut a notch for every day. I shall stitch a new coat for Agrippa, and take him with me under my arm. Where art thou going? To the Cathedral?"

"Nay, I had best keep away from the Cathedral. I am going to speak with the bridge warden, for a mischievous loon has knocked away a bit of the monument to Master Gervase, in his chapel on the bridge, and they have sent up here for some one to repair it."

Elyas had recovered so marvellously that scarcely any trace of his severe attack was noticeable except to those who knew him best. He did not mount on ladders, but in other respects had resumed work, and had been frequently at the Cathedral in consultation with the bishop, who was delighted to have his right-hand adviser again. Of course he might, had he so pleased, have seen the corbels, finished or unfinished, which were being executed by his own men, but he had determined to wait for the general view, and to give his voice as to the best with the other judges. Meanwhile, his interest was intense, and he could talk of little, so that Prothasy, between husband, child, journeymen, and prentice, had some reason for vowing that she could not get a sensible word on any subject from a creature in the house.

And this excitement increased as Lammas Day drew nearer. Roger said little, but his pale face grew paler, his lips more tightly set, and there was a feverish light in his eyes which spoke of a fire within. Franklyn, who was one of the last, worked stolidly on, very much as he had been used to work in the yard, taking it as a matter of business to be got through fairly and conscientiously, and knowing the value of his work so well that he was not troubled with fear of failure. Wat was wild with conjectures, thinking most of all about Hugh, but also devoured by a wish that he had given more care to the beginning of his work, and ready, if other justice failed, to break Roger's head sooner than allow him to enjoy the fruit of his wickedness.

The last of Joan's notches was made at last, and Lammas Day dawned, fair, and hot, and tranquil. Joan was up with the lark, looking very sweet and maidenly in her new blue kirtle, and seeing that the green branches were ready which she had brought in the day before in order to deck the house as soon as either of their own workers was declared to be first.

"Saving Roger," she announced. "There shall be no decking for Roger."

Her father rebuked her for her lack of charity, but he himself looked uneasy, for he could not forget that Roger had been one of his family, and treated as a son, and it pained him to the heart to suppose that he could be guilty of such baseness as that of which he was suspected. He hoped with all his heart that his work would prove him innocent.

On all Sundays and holy days the officers of the city, the mayor, the sheriff, the aldermen, the wardens of Exe bridge, and at times the members of the guilds, were bound to attend the bishop to St. Peter's Church. But this day had in it the promise of an especial ceremony, one in which the bishop took deep interest. The office of nones being ended in the Lady Chapel, the procession was to enter the choir, where six corbels, for the first time uncovered, were to meet the eyes of the spectators. And this being so, the usual number was greatly increased, and presented a splendour of colour which at this time can hardly be realised. The ecclesiastical dress was extremely gorgeous, and here were bishop, dean, and chapter in full robes, the mayor and aldermen not far behind in magnificence, with a great preponderance of blue in the civil dresses, and robes lined with fur (or vair). The guilds added their brilliancy of colour, the craftsmen wearing their distinctive dress, and as the procession swept round into the choir, the sunlight falling brilliantly through the stained glass windows, in themselves one of the wonders of the time, and as all the beauty of the choir revealed itself, the grey Purbeck stone contrasting delicately with the somewhat yellowish tinge of the walls, the scene was one of amazing splendour, and the burst of song which broke forth as the singers raised the psalms of degrees, told that it had touched an answering chord in the hearts of the people. Most of the great families of the county had sent some representative. There were Grenvils and Fitz-Ralffes, Greenways of Brixham, Bartholomew and Joan Giffard of Halsberry, Sir Roger Hale, and numbers of ladies wearing long trains, and gold-embroidered mantles, and on their heads veils; while the black or grey frocks of the friars from the neighbouring priories gave the necessary relief to colour which might otherwise have been too dazzling. Lammas Day, moreover, was the day of Exeter fair, which added to the concourse.

But Joan had no eyes for any of this great assemblage. She could just catch sight of Hugh moving on in his place among the guild apprentices, and she could see that his head was bent, and knew that his hands would be knotted together, as was ever the way with him when he was feeling strong emotion. But even Joan, clasping her mother's hand, and sending her heart out to him in sympathy, little knew what a storm of feeling was surging up in the young man's heart. His father had never seemed so near. He understood, as he had never understood before, the wood-carver's longing to see his name famous; he understood, too, that higher longing which had moved him before his death. In this work of his Hugh had resigned the ambition for his own honour and glory, for he honestly believed that all he had done had been to carry out his master's design, and was unaware of what his own power had added. Nor was he going in with hope that even this execution would surpass that of the others. He knew his own shortcomings, they often seemed to him to be absolutely destructive, and he imagined all the excellences he had dreamed of distributed among the others. But at this moment it scarcely troubled him; what he felt was the solemnity and beauty of the scene, the glory of the building, the greatness of having been permitted to help in making it beautiful; he raised his head and a light shone in his eyes, for he knew that his father's deepest yearnings would have been satisfied. There were the six corbels, fair and fresh from the carvers' hands, the rich stone with its almost golden tints adding the charm of colour to the nobility of the work; there were the clustered columns, massive, yet light, and high up the glorious lines of vaulting. Right on one of the corbels—it was Wat's—struck a shaft of sunlight, and as the long procession crossed this gleam, all the brilliant colours were intensified, and the upturned faces of the little acolytes looked like those of child-angels. The procession did not pause. It swept through the choir and out of the side gate, still chanting the psalms of degrees, till the voices died away, and the choir was filled by those who had come to see Bishop Bitton's work thus nobly carried out.

Hugh did not return—he could not, though Franklyn had almost dragged him by force, and told him that Gervase had asked for him. He shook off Wat, who begged him at least to come outside and see the horses and trappings of the Lord of Pomeroy who had come in from his castle of Biry, a castle much renowned in the county, and who was famous for his success in the jousts. Here was his coal-black horse Paladin, whose sire he had brought back from the Crusades, and the noblest mastiff Wat had ever beheld, and such a jester as—

But Hugh was gone.

His heart was too full for speech with anyone. He had always been a self-restrained boy who, when deeply moved, liked to be alone, and sometimes vexed faithful Joan by escaping even her sympathy. And now he felt as if only the woods could shelter him. He loved them deeply, he went to them for inspiration for his work; he went now when he wanted he knew not what, for it was neither comfort nor rejoicing, only an over-fulness of heart. He could not have told whether he had failed or succeeded, for the perception of something higher than success had touched him, and it was this which drove him forth into the solitudes of the woods.

When an hour had passed the throng had left the choir, and the bishop and chapter, together with all the officers of the Guild of Stonemasons, came in once more to pronounce upon the work.

Bishop Bitton was strangely moved. He saw before him a work, not yet, it is true, complete, yet, for the length of his episcopate, marvellous; a work in which he had loyally carried out the lines laid down by his predecessor. His health was failing, and the conviction was strong upon him that not many years of life remained to him. He, too, like Hugh, would have thankfully passed these hours alone, but for him it was not possible; he must listen to the kindly congratulations of the dean, the half-veiled spite of the precentor, the unintelligent praise of others. But all the while his heart was sending up its thankful *Nunc dimittis*.

And Gervase? His thoughts were perhaps the most mingled of any, and the most unselfish. To him the desire of his soul had not been granted. He had been forced to relinquish it to others, yet he could rejoice ungrudgingly, giving full meed of praise and admiration. And, indeed, the corbels were of noble beauty. From one to another the groups passed, pausing to note each characteristic, and so fair was each that it was hard to gather judgment.

With one exception.

Unanimously Hugh's corbel, or, as it was rather called, Gervase's, was declared the best both in design and execution. It varied from the others, in which the whole mass was formed of leafage, while this was broken by curved lines round which the foliage grouped itself, and nothing could have been more admirable than the freedom of the lines, and the grace and spontaneousness of the design. The bishop, after standing long to gaze at it, turned and stretched out his hand to Elyas.

"This is a proud day for thee, friend," he said heartily, "for by common consent thy design is held so far to surpass all the others that there is not one can come near it. And thy prentice hath ably carried out thy views."

"He hath done more, my lord," said Elyas, quickly; "the parts of the design which delight you all are his, not mine. Never saw I aught more enriched than my thoughts in his hands. There is none other to equal it, that I allow, but the credit belongs to Hugh Bassett, not to Elyas Gervase."

The bishop looked incredulously at him, and others who had gathered round shook their heads.

"'Tis impossible," said the bishop. "Bethink thee, goodman, the lad, though clever in his craft, is youngest of all the workmen. Thou hast ever favoured him, and maybe art scarcely aware how much thy skill hath aided him."

"My lord, no one knows better than myself how much and how little."

But Gervase, to his great distress, found that his protestations were disregarded. Some, like the bishop, believed that in his zeal for his apprentice, in whom it was known that he took more than usual interest, he did not remember all the advice he had given; others were perhaps willing to yield the first place to one who as a leading burgess was greatly respected in the city, and whose illness had raised the ready sympathy of all, while 'twould have been another matter to put a lad—younger than any—there. Hardly one was there who would give the credit of more than an excellent execution to Hugh, though Elyas grew hot and fevered with his efforts to persuade them of the truth, and could scarcely keep his usually even temper under the congratulations which poured upon him, and which made him feel like a traitor, though a most unwilling traitor, to Hugh. The master of the guild, who was an old man and deaf, especially pooh-poohed his remonstrances.

"I mind me, goodman, that when thou wast a prentice, and an idle one, I ever maintained that the day would come when thou wouldst do us credit, and thy father, honest man, he cast up his hands, and 'Alack, Master Garland,' quoth he, 'the day is long in coming!' 'The day is long in coming,' those were his very words. What dost thou say? My hearing is not so sharp as it was—thy prentice? Ay, ay, the lad hath done well, very well, but anyone can see whose was the band that directed his."

"Beshrew me if they will not soon persuade me that I am an old dotard, knowing neither what I say nor what I do!" cried Elyas angrily to his fellow-warden. "I shall hear next that I have carved the *surs* myself! Hugh shall show them what he can do when he has his next corbel to carry out alone. I will not even look at it."

"It is said that that he will not have," replied John Hamlyn drily.

"Not? And wherefore?"

"The judges maintain it should be given to one whose corbel has been solely his own work. I have withdrawn from the competition, having much to execute for my Lord of Pomeroy, and some say it should fall to thy man Wat, whose scratching dog is marvellously well managed, but, unless I am mistaken, the greater part hold to another man of thine—Roger. His design is most delicately intricate."

Gervase was greatly disturbed.

"I would have had naught to do with the matter had I believed in such unfairness," he said, with heat. "I would I had never asked the poor lad to give up his own work to do mine, nor hampered him with my design!"

"Take it not so much to heart, goodman."

"Nay, but I must, I must. 'Tis the injustice that weighs on me, and shame that Hugh should be served so scurvily. Roger! I shall speak presently with the bishop."

He redoubled his earnestness, speaking, indeed, with so much decision, that the bishop was impressed. But, as he said, the feeling among the judges was very strong, and he did not himself believe that anything could be advanced that would turn them. There was, moreover, a conviction that Hugh was young enough to wait, and therefore, though a doubt might exist, they were opposed to giving him the benefit of the doubt. Nor could anything which Elyas advanced shake their determination. Something, it was true, was whispered as to an ugly story of a ladder, but the thing had never been proved against Roger, and except among the workmen had been forgotten. And the workmen were not the judges.

Ladders were now procured, and the corbels were minutely examined. Nothing, it was freely owned, approached the beauty of Hugh's, and no other exceeded it in admirable workmanship. If both design and execution had been his, there could have been no question; as it was—

"The obstinate fools!" growled Gervase, under his breath.

Finally the workers were themselves admitted, Wat coming in eager and triumphant, with the certainty that Hugh's success was assured, and Roger pale, nervous, glancing furtively from side to side, as if trying to read his fate in the faces round. Wat strode joyously to Gervase.

"Where is Hugh?" asked his master.

"Gone off, sir, in one of his solitary moods. But Mistress Prothasy is preparing a rare feast in his honour." Then, as he noticed Gervase's grave face, he stopped and stared at him.

"Ay, Wat, it is even so," said Elyas, bitterly.

"These wise men will have it that the *surs* is my designing, and that Hugh hath but carved it. Heardest thou ever such injustice? I may talk, and they pay no more heed than if I were—thy dog whom thou hast set up there. And, by the mass," he added kindly, "thou hast done him marvellous well, and there has been a talk of thy having the other corbel."

"I would not have taken it," said Wat hotly.

"I had rather it had been in thy hands than in Roger's."

"Roger, goodman!" cried Wat, starting forward. "Not that traitor?"

"Peace, peace! I am as grieved as thou, but we know not that he is a traitor."

"Ay, by my troth, but I do!" Wat persisted, "and so shall they all. Where is Warden Hamlyn?"

"Nay, I know not. It is not long since he was here," answered Elyas, surprised. "What hast thou in thy mad head? Bethink thee, Wat, we do Hugh but harm to bring charges which we cannot prove, and though it was a foul act to cut that ladder—"

"It is not the ladder, goodman," cried Wat, earnestly. "Thou wast ill, and we did not tell thee of the other villainy. Hast thou looked at Roger's corbel?"

"Ay," with surprise.

"Is it new to thee?"

"Nay, I seemed to know every twist of the ivy. But I thought—my memory plays me scurvy tricks since my illness—I thought, though I could not call it to mind, that Roger must have brought it to me to ask my counsel. Surely it was so?"

"Nay, goodman, when did Roger ask thy counsel? It was Hugh who brought it to thee, and, knowing Roger's evil disposition, we were ever on the watch against eavesdropping and prying. But the day thou wast taken with thy sickness Hugh forgot it, and Roger stole the design. And now! But he shall not gain his end," cried Wat, fiercely. "Goodman, where shall I be most likely to find Master Hamlyn?"

"Go and ask his head man there. But what good can he do thee?"

Wat, however, was already off, blaming himself bitterly that in the excitement of the morning, and his undoubted certainty that Hugh was secure of being first, he had omitted to remind the warden of what he held in trust. To add to his dismay, he could get no tidings of John Hamlyn. Each person he asked said he had been there but now, and must be somewhere close at hand, but he never arrived nearer, though he scoured the Cathedral from end to end, and brought upon himself a severe rating from the precentor. Then in despair he rushed off to Hamlyn's house, where he met the warden's wife and daughter setting forth to find out what was going on at the Cathedral. Even in the midst of his anxiety, Wat was suddenly seized with the conviction that Margaret Hamlyn, with her dark eyes and her primrose kirtle, was the sweetest maiden he had ever beheld, and she showed so much desire to help him, and was so very hopeful as to their finding her father, that before ten minutes were over he had not the smallest doubt on the matter.

Nevertheless, nothing could be heard of Hamlyn. Wat met Joan, who had been waiting and watching for Hugh until she could keep away no longer, and was come to seek Elyas with a little bundle tucked under her arm, from which she allowed a quaint wizened face to peep at Wat. Her confidence that all was well for Hugh, and her pretty pleasure in bringing Agrippa to join in his triumph, were so great that Wat had not the heart to damp them by telling her of the untoward turn events had taken; he only said impatiently that things were not yet settled, and that Hugh was an ass to go and bury himself in the green woods instead of coming forward with the others.

"Do they want him?" asked Joan stopping.

"Nay, I know not that they want him," returned Wat, "but he should be there."

"Then I shall go back and watch for him," she said resolutely. "Mother is busy with the supper and might not see him. I know where he is gone, and he must come in by the North Gate, and I will get the keeper to let me sit there and wait. I will bring him, Wat, never fear."

But as the minutes flew and nothing was seen of John Hamlyn, Wat began to wish that he had done nothing to draw Hugh to a place where he would only find his own just meeds passed over, and evil-doing triumphant. Gervase stood apart from his friends; he was sick at heart, feeling as if he had been the cause of all that had happened to Hugh, from his desire to see his own designs carried out. Perhaps he had not yet regained his usual healthy buoyancy, for all looked black; he felt strangely unable to influence those with whom his word had always carried weight, but most of all he grieved for Roger's treachery.

Presently there was a little stir among the knot of judges, and Franklyn, who was near them, came over to Elyas, and whispered—

"It is all decided, goodman."

"For Roger?"

"Ay. It should have been Hugh's to my thinking, for the lad hath surpassed us all. But they vow it is thy design."

"Ay, they know better than I do," said Elyas bitterly. "See they are calling him up."

Roger, indeed, was moving towards the group with an air which had gained assurance since he first came into the choir. The old master of the guild spoke in his quavering voice.

"Of these carvings which have been placed here to the honour of God and His holy Apostle, it is held that thine, Roger Brewer, is the most complete. Thou art therefore permitted to undertake the carving of another corbel, and to make choice of which thou wilt for thyself."

Somebody started forward.

"Sir, it is no design of his; he is a false braggart, and stole it from Hugh Bassett."

A great confusion arose, angry looks were turned on Wat, and the bishop moved forward and raised his hands.

"Methinks, masters, you forget in whose house we be. That is a grave accusation. Hast thou answer to make, Roger Brewer?"

"Ay, my lord," said Roger, standing boldly forward. "I say it is a foul lie, and that he is ever seeking to do me a mischief, and I demand his proofs."

"That hast thou a right to require. Where are the proofs?"

"My lord, I have them not, but—"

Roger broke in with a scornful smile.

"Said I not so? You see, my lord."

In his turn he was interrupted by a grave voice, "My lord, the proofs are here. I but waited to see whether he would have the grace to withdraw his claim;" and John Hamlyn, stepping forward, raised a broad board so that it might be seen of all. "Will the judges say whether this design is the same as that carved by Roger Brewer?"

THE ORIGINAL OF ROGER'S CORBEL.   p. 278.

There was a close examination and comparison, at the end of which the master, after consultation with the others, raised his head.

"It is undoubtedly the same."

"Now," continued Hamlyn, turning the board, "there is writing here, which you and I, my masters, cannot fathom. Maybe my lord bishop will have the grace to construe it for us."

The bishop advanced, and in a clear voice read, "Hugh Bassett, Saint George's Day, A.D. 1303."

"Wat, repeat thy story," said Hamlyn quietly. "I have kept thy proof safely, though truly until this day I knew not what it was worth."

Thus adjured Wat, though finding it hard to keep down his excitement, told what he had to tell straightforwardly and well. He related how, having his suspicions raised, he had warned Hugh to beware of Roger, and how on the day of Gervase's illness the design had disappeared. That then it had come into his mind to advise Hugh to draw it again, to place a date upon it and give it into Mistress Prothasy's keeping. That she had held it safely until Master John Hamlyn took it from her, and that from the day of the date Hugh had never had it in his hands nor so much as seen it.

This was all, but with the board before them, it was evidence which could hardly be strengthened, and if more were needed, Roger's white, fear-stricken face supplied it. There was a significant silence, broken at last by the bishop's voice.

"Where is Hugh Bassett?" he asked.

"Now, in good sooth, was ever anything so foolish as that he should have hidden himself as he hath done?" whispered the provoked Wat to his neighbour. But at that moment the circle of interested citizens opened, and Hugh, looking flushed and disturbed, came forward, while behind him were Elyas and Joan.

"Hugh Bassett," said the bishop, pointing to the board, "is that thy work?"

"Ay, my lord," he answered in a low voice.

Again a pause.

"Thou hast heard the relation of its keeping?"

"Nay, my lord, I have but this moment come into the church."

"Let us hear what thou hast to say."

Hugh told his story, which agreed in every respect with that already related. While it was telling the miserable Roger tried to slip away, but at a sign from Hamlyn two members of the guild silently placed themselves on either side. Then Elyas stepped forward.

"I speak with pain, my lord," he said, "for Roger Brewer is my journeyman and hath been my apprentice, but to keep silence were to sin against this holy place. My sickness hath made me oblivious, but the ivy is strangely familiar to me, and I mind me that Hugh ever brought his designs to show me, while Roger had no such habit. Moreover, although you have refused to listen to what I said as to the corbel carved by Hugh Bassett, I would urge upon you to consider it viewed in the light of what has now passed."

He was listened to in absolute silence, and presently bishop, chapter, and judges retired to consult, while the others waited, and Elyas, whose kind heart was deeply grieved for Roger, drew off and knelt in prayer.

The consultation was not long, the judges came back, and once again the old master delivered their judgment.

"It having been proved that Hugh Bassett rather than Roger Brewer designed the ivy corbel, it is declared that his work standeth first in merit, and he is granted the carving of another corbel, and the choice of pillar."

Had it not been church Wat would have leapt high in the air.

No more was said, for it was not the fitting place in which to deal with Roger's misdoing, which would be the work of the guild, but he was removed by the two men who had him in charge, and those who were left pressed round Hugh to seize his hand. He had known nothing of the first acts of the drama, but his day in the quiet woods was no ill preparation for this moment of success. Elyas came up and laid a broad hand on his shoulder, and Joan slipped hers into Hugh's.

"Come home and tell mother," she whispered.

But when they at length got outside the Cathedral door a strange and unexpected sight met them, for Wat, who was a great favourite with the apprentices, had rushed out, and in an incredibly short time had gathered a large number together, and marshalled them at the door to greet Hugh when he came. There was no need to bid them cheer; the tidings that one of their number had gained so great an honour raised them to wild enthusiasm, and made them forget their usual rivalries; they pressed round the Cathedral door, and when he came out, literally flung themselves upon him, shouting at the top of their voices, and waving sticks or anything which came to hand; finally, in spite of all he could do, seizing and bearing him off in their arms, carrying him in triumph through Broad Gate out into the High Street, and joined by fresh boys at every turn of the road. Citizens ran out on hearing the tumult, the watchmen caught up their staves and hurried forth, the Pomeroy and Ralegh retainers cheered them on, all the windows and balconies were quickly filled with women who laughed and waved their hands, and the mayor himself, so far from showing any anger, stood in a balcony and flung down largesse upon the shouting lads. Nothing would suffice, but to carry Hugh all down the steep street to Exe bridge, where, near seven years before, he had come in under such different circumstances, and, hot and shamefaced as he was, he could not but think of this, and scarce knew where he was for the thinking.

Hot he might be, but there was no persuading them, to put him down, and up the street they went again, cheering still, and between the old houses, until they stopped at Gervase's door, where Elyas himself stood with Prothasy, and Joan clapping her hands with all her might. And there was more shouting and rejoicing when Elyas bid all the prentices to a feast in the meadows on St. Bartholomew's Day, his own house not having space for such a number.

They separated at last, and reluctantly, after such a shrill burst of cheering as rang through the old city, and Hugh, who felt as if it were all some strange exciting dream, was thankful to find himself alone with those good friends to whom he owed his present fortune. Elyas put his hands on his shoulders, and looked into the clear eyes, now on a level with his own.

"Thy father could not have been more glad than I," he said simply.

"I would I could thank thee, goodman," said Hugh, in an unsteady voice, "for all comes from thee."

"Nay, neither me nor thee, but from One Who gave the gift. And thou—thou hast kept covenant."

"I looked not for anything like this."

"Doubtless it hath been a little upsetting," said Elyas, with a smile, "but it hath made Wat as happy as a king. Never was a more faithful friend, or that had less thought for himself. I verily believe he never cared for his own work; he did his best simply, and there left it. 'Tis a rare nature. Alack, alack, I would poor Roger had been as free from self-seeking!"

"Goodman," said Hugh, hesitatingly, "hast thou heard aught of Roger?"

"I went to the Guildhall from the Cathedral and saw him. I might have been a stranger and an enemy," Elyas added, sighing, "for all I could get from him."

"Might I speak for him? Would they hearken? I love him not, in good sooth," said Hugh frankly, "and I know not what I might have felt if he had succeeded; but 'tis easy to forgive when he hath done no one harm but himself. Maybe, sir, he might do better if he had another chance?"

"That may not be here," said the warden, gravely. "Some were for flinging him into gaol, but they hearkened to me so far that he will be but heavily fined, and sent from the city, never to return. Speak not of him. I would rather not grieve on this day. But first, before I hand thee over to Joan, who doth not yet feel she hath had her share, first tell me which corbel thou wilt choose? I counsel the one opposite to that thou hast finished. There is no fairer position for showing the beauty of thy work."

But Hugh shook his head.

"Nay, I have set my heart upon another."

"And which is that?"

"It is the first which was allotted to me, that on the left as you enter the choir, where the rood-screen is to stand."

"That!" said Gervase, disappointed. "Bethink thee, Hugh, it is not so well seen as any of the others."

"Thou hast ever taught us, goodman, that we should give as good work to the parts which are not seen as to the rest," said Hugh, mischievously. "But, in truth, I have thought so much of that corbel, and let my fancies play about it so long, that it seems more mine own than any. Let me have it."

"Nay, thou must choose for thyself, for none of us can gainsay thee."

"And the other should be kept for thee. I know the guild would have thy work before any man's."

Gervase's eyes brightened.

"With our Lady and the Blessed Babe—I know not, I know not, I would liefer have it in thy hands."

"I hold to my own."

"Father, father," cried Joan, running in, "mother bids me ask whether thou hast told Nicholas Harding to come and help her with the tables? And she saith Hal will drive her demented unless thou find some errand for him to do."

Such a feast as Prothasy had prepared! And to it came John Hamlyn, his wife, and daughter, and Wat, contriving to sit next to Mistress Margaret, was able to tell her the whole tale, which seemed to her most marvellously interesting. Also she questioned him much about his own corbel, and was amazed to think that it should have been a neighbour's dog which he had set up, and would fain see for herself the unconscious Spot who had been thus immortalised. And afterwards she spoke very prettily to Wat's mother, who had come in from her farm, a proud woman to think what her son had done, and gazing at him as if no mother had ever another such.

But the happiest perhaps was Joan. With Agrippa in her arms, she sat next to Hugh, and could whisper to him from time to time, and listen to what was said, and rejoice with all her faithful little heart. Never apprentice had won such honour, and never, said Elyas strongly to John Hamlyn, could one deserve it better. And in the midst of the feast came a messenger bringing Hugh a gift from the bishop, a reliquary of goodly workmanship.

Such a day, as Joan said that evening with a sigh of happiness, had never been before!

Chapter Sixteen.

The Second Corbel.

There is little more to tell. My story is like a web of knitting, and now the point is reached where the stitches have to be cast off, and the work left. It has been no more than a tale of apprenticeship, and Hugh's man's life was but just beginning. Yet those years are enough to tell us what the rest was likely to be.

For months he toiled at the second corbel, and in these months passed out of his apprenticeship and became journeyman. Master Gervase was wont to say that the lad was in a fair way to be spoilt, for the story of that Lammas Day got abroad, as stories did in those days, carried back by the Pomeroy retainers to Biry, and by the Raleghs to Street Ralegh, and caught at by the wandering minstrels and story-tellers, who were the great bearers of news about the country, and ever on the watch for some gossip which they might retail at fair or castle, where it travelled from the buttery hatch to my lady's closet, and lost naught in the telling. The town had been crowded by these strangers at the time of the corbel incident, the annual fair being held on Lammas Day, so that there was fine opportunity for spreading of news; and when the families from the great houses in the county came into the city, they must needs go to the Cathedral to see the carving which had caused so much stir, and those who had work of their own going on would have had Hugh Bassett to carry it out. But nothing would draw him from the corbel.

"I marvel at the lad," said John Hamlyn one day to his fellow-warden; "he seems to care little for the over-praise he gets. 'Twould turn my Ralph's head."

"His father's training has borne fruit," answered Elyas. "Hugh gave up his own fancies, and held by what he had learnt to be duty; now he yet thinks of the duty, and not of the glory to himself. He is as good to me as any son could be."

"And may be thy son in good earnest?"

"With all my heart," said Gervase cheerfully. "But that must bide awhile."

Hamlyn looked him up and down.

"Thou art as hale, goodman, as ever thou wert before thy sickness."

"Ay, thank God! When the spring comes and the cold of winter is over I shall fall to work upon the *surs*."

"Best make speed, for the old master can hardly last much longer, and it will not become thy dignity to be seen on a ladder when thou art in his place."

"Tut, tut, man! were I King of England it would become me to work for the King of kings. But this is idle telling. Wilt come into the yard? That malapert Hal is like to drive William Franklyn out of his wits with his idle pranks, and I am ever needed to keep the peace."

"And yet in sooth, goodman, thy prentices do thee credit—I would mine were of the same value," said Hamlyn, with a sigh and a thought of his son Ralph. "I really believe their thick pates can hold naught but the desire to break those of others. Now there is that man of thine, Wat—he," Hamlyn paused, "he is a likely fellow?"

"As good a lad as ever breathed," returned Gervase heartily. Then he looked at the other warden and smiled. "Thou didst fling out something just now of my having a son in Hugh. Maybe thou hast a thought of finding a son thyself and more quickly?"

"I'd as lief know what like the lad is," said Hamlyn gruffly. "He greatly favours our house, and on Holy Cross Day brought nuts enough to Madge to feed a wood full of squirrels."

"He is a boy in his play yet," answered Elyas, "but I have marked him closely, and he hath in him the making of a true man. I tell thee, neighbour, thou wouldst do well for thy daughter's happiness to give her Wat for a husband."

Hamlyn protested that it had not come to this yet, but it was easy to see that he was well inclined to the young stonemason, and that if Wat's fancy lasted, which at this time appeared probable, he might win pretty Margaret for his wife. There was a squire in my Lord of Devon's meiné who was desirous to marry her, but Hamlyn had no liking for what he called a roystering cut-throat trade, much preferring one of his own craft, even though his daughter might have aspired to a richer suitor. Wat's simple loyalty to his friend and total absence of self-seeking had struck them all, and his corbel was greatly admired, so that the Prideaux family in seeking someone to carve a rich monument had expressed a hope that he would be chosen for the work.

Of Roger nothing had been heard. He had gone forth, forbidden to return, and though Gervase's kind heart had yearned for a word which might show repentance, and give him an excuse for helping him, the word never came.

The winter was a sharp one, so sharp that Hugh's carving was somewhat hindered by the extreme cold. And just at the New Year Agrippa died.

He had grown old and feeble, no longer able to swing about from rafter to beam as in old days, most content to lie near the fire, wrapped in a piece of warm scarlet Flemish wool which they provided for him, and in his old age showing yet more markedly his likes and dislikes. Never had he done more than tolerate Prothasy, and now, when she came near him, he chattered and scolded with all his weak might. Franklyn, one or two of the men, and prentice Hal he detested equally, but there was a new prentice, Gilbert, whom he permitted to stroke him. Joan he loved, saving always when Hugh was near. For him he had a passionate devotion which was pathetic. When he was in the room he was never content unless Hugh took him up, and he was jealous even of Joan if she withdrew Hugh's attention. Yet in spite of his spoilt and irritable ways all the household cared for the quaint little creature, and it was Gervase himself who came down to the Cathedral, when they were singing nones in the Lady Chapel, to fetch Hugh, who, his fingers having grown stiff over his corbel with the bitter cold, had given it up for the day, and was working under Franklyn's directions at some of the larger work which yet remained to be finished in the choir.

"Joan would have thee home to see Agrippa," said the warden, laying his hand as he loved to do on Hugh's shoulder; "the poor beast is sorely sick—unto death, if I mistake not."

It did not take Hugh many minutes to dash through St. Martin's Gate into the High Street and his master's house. Joan called to him the moment she heard his voice, and he found her in much distress, kneeling close to the fire on which she had piled as many logs as she could. There under his scarlet covering lay poor Agrippa at the last gasp, but still able to recognise his master with the old look of love, and the stretching forth his poor little shrunk paw. Hugh flung himself down by his side, heaping endearments upon him, while Joan held back lest her presence by Hugh should stir the little creature's anger. It was over the next moment. One loving piteous look, one movement as though to raise himself towards his master, and the eyes glazed and the limbs stiffened, and Hugh's faithful little companion for more than seven years was gone.

Joan sobbed bitterly, and Hugh was more moved than he would have cared to let anyone but her see. They both knelt on by his side, till Hugh rose and drew her to her feet.

"Poor Agrippa! He has had a happy home, thanks to thee. Thou wert his first protector, Joan."

She looked up and smiled through her tears.

"When thou wast so frighted at mother that thou must needs break thy indentures and run away! Father hath often told me of it. 'Twas well it was father, and that he was able to keep it from coming to the guild. But to think thou didst not know mother better."

She was a wise little maiden, capable as was Prothasy, and with as warm affections, but a gentler manner of showing them. And from her father she had inherited his gift of imagination and love of beauty, so that in the greenwood not Hugh himself had a quicker eye for the loveliness of interlacing trees, or the fancies of the foliage, and as he sometimes told her, she should have been a boy and a stone-carver. The art of painting, save in missals, can scarcely be said to have existed in those days, when all beautiful materials, glow of colour, and picturesqueness of line, were at its disposal, and art was forced to take refuge in architecture, which it carried to its noblest height, or, with women, in exquisite embroideries.

Joan had smiled, but she was very sad for Agrippa, and nothing would comfort her but hearing of Hugh's progress with his *surs*, when 'twould be finished and she might see it.

"It should have been done by now," said Hugh, "but this biting cold stiffens my fingers so that I cannot venture on the delicate parts. Come, now, Joan, what sayest thou to thy birthday—Candlemas Day?"

She clapped her hands.

"In good sooth. And if father is still better—which Our Lady grant!—he will begin his work that month."

Elyas, indeed, showed no signs of his past sickness, and as the leech, when Prothasy spoke to him, assured her that malignant influences no longer threatened, she was greatly comforted. He said himself that his memory failed, but no one else saw any unusual signs of this not uncommon complaint, and there was little doubt that he would be elected its master by the guild, which some two hundred years later was to stretch itself so far as to incorporate together "Carpenters, Masons, Joiners, and Glaziers and Painters."

There was no such excitement on Candlemas Day as there had been five months before, for nothing hung on the uncovering of Hugh's carving beyond learning whether his second work would equal the promise of his first, and this to the outer world meant little. To his own little world, and to the bishop, it meant much. The fame of his first work had come through difficulties and by a roundabout fashion; in this that he had now completed no one could either rightly or wrongly claim a part. When therefore, after the Hours, the bishop and a few of his clergy entered the choir, they found a knot of guild officers there, and all Gervase's household, together with Hamlyn's wife and daughters, and a few workmen who had not cared to keep holiday.

"No greenwood for thee, Hugh, to-day," Elyas had said, and the young man was there himself, looking gravely content, and not, as Mistress Hamlyn expressed it, in the least puffed with pride.

At a sign from the bishop, he mounted the ladder and drew off the wrapping cloths.

Much had been seen during the carving, but now for the first time the work was beheld in its full beauty, and from the group there went up an irrepressible murmur of admiration.

It was a group of figures. At the top Our Lord and His Mother in glory; below, a single figure of Saint Cecilia drawing music from an instrument shaped something like a lute, but played with a bow; over her head, inclined gently to the left, a little angel hovered. The grace and sweetness of her attitude, the fall of the draperies, the delicacy of the workmanship, raised the beholders into enthusiasm, and though the corbel was not so prominent as the others, something in the angle in which it was seen, and the manner in which it stood out against the outer nave, added to the effect of beauty.

Hugh had modestly stood aside while the examination went on, but Joan had stolen to him and slipped her hand in his, and now Elyas turned and embraced him.

"Hugh," he said, "I am proud to count thee as my son."

Wat was there, too, absolutely beaming with delight, and seizing Hugh's hand as if he would wring it off.

"Said I not, said I not,"—he began, and then, "no one can say aught against thy work now; but, Hugh—"

"Ay?"

"Couldst not carve a Saint Margaret as well as a Saint Cecilia? Prithee—"

But here his request was broken off by a message that the Lord Bishop would speak with Hugh Bassett.

Bishop Bitton, who had aged fast of late, was leaning on the arm of one of his priests, but his face was lit with that fire of enthusiasm which could always be stirred in him by aught that was good or great. As Hugh came up, he raised his hand, and the young man dropped on his knee to receive the blessing.

And as, deeply moved, he rose and stood on one side, it seemed to him that his father's dying voice stole softly upon his ears—

"Not for thyself, but for the glory of God."

Milton Keynes UK
Ingram Content Group UK Ltd.
UKHW050037220624
444555UK00004B/435